"Woman, do I look like a goddamned fish? Because the last time I checked, I didn't have a tail. And I sure as hell don't have gills. I am a man. *Mer. Man.* So you'd damned well better get used to it."

— Shane, the Merman

OTHER WORKS BY MIMI JEAN PAMFILOFF

FATE BOOK (New Adult Suspense)
FATE BOOK TWO (New Adult Suspense)
HAPPY PANTS CAFÉ
(a Romantic Comedy/Contemporary Romance)

THE KING TRILOGY

King's (Book 1)
King for a Day (Book 2)
King of Me (Book 3)

THE ACCIDENTALLY YOURS SERIES

Accidentally in Love with…a God?
Accidentally Married to…a Vampire?
Sun God Seeks…Surrogate?
Accidentally…Evil? (a Novella)
Vampires Need Not…Apply?
Accidentally…Cimil? (a Novella)
Accidentally…Over? (Series Finale)

COMING SOON

MERMADMEN (Book 2, the Mermen Trilogy)
IMMORTAL MATCHMAKERS, INC. (Book 1)
MERCILESS (Book 3, the Mermen Trilogy)

ISBN-10: 0990304876
ISBN-13: 978-0-9903048-7-6

Cover Design: EarthlyCharms.com

Editing: Latoya Smith and Pauline Nolet

Interior design: WriteIntoPrint.com

MERMEN

Book 1
The Mermen Trilogy

Mimi Jean Pamfiloff

Mimi Boutique Imprint

Like "FREE" Pirated Books?
Then Ask Yourself This Question:
WHO ARE THESE PEOPLE I'M HELPING?

What sort of person or organization would put up a website that uses stolen work (or encourages its users to share stolen work) in order to make money for themselves, either through website traffic or direct sales?

Haven't you ever wondered?

Putting up thousands of pirated books onto a website or creating those anonymous ebook file sharing sites takes time and resources. Quite a lot, actually.

So who are these people? Do you think they're decent, ethical people with good intentions? Why do they set up camp anonymously in countries where they can't easily be touched? And the money they make from advertising every time you go to their website, or through selling stolen work, **what are they using it for?**

The answer is you don't know.

They could be terrorists, organized criminals, or just greedy bastards. But one thing we DO know is that **THEY ARE CRIMINALS** who don't care about you, your family, or me and mine.

And their intentions can't be good.

And every time you illegally share or download a book, YOU ARE HELPING these people. Meanwhile, people like me, who work to support a family and children, are left wondering why anyone would condone this.

So please, please ask yourself who YOU are HELPING when you support ebook piracy and then ask yourself who you are HURTING.

And for those who legally purchased or borrowed or obtained my work from a reputable retailer (not sure, just ask me!) muchas thank yous! You rock.

The unauthorized reproduction or distribution of a copyrighted work is illegal. Criminal copyright infringement, including infringement without monetary gain, is investigated by the FBI and is punishable by fines and federal imprisonment.

Dedicated to Latoya Smith.

Because saying thank you for all that
you've done just isn't enough.

MERMEN

CHAPTER ONE

Bump. Bump.

"What the fuck was that?" Twenty-nine-year-old Liv Stratton sat up in her sagging life raft, trying to stay conscious.

Bump.

There it is again. Liv's eyes skimmed the perimeter but saw nothing. Well, except the warm March sun glaring off an endless stretch of eerily calm North Pacific. *Water, water everywhere, but not a drop to—*

From the corner of her eye, she caught a splash about a hundred yards out. It appeared to be...

Wait. She leaned forward. *Is that...is that? No. You did not just see a naked man swimming.* The dehydration was playing tricks on her, making her believe she'd just seen a tanned, muscular form floating on his back, everything on display.

You're hallucinating again. Liv sighed and flopped back onto the raft, shoving her sticky dark hair over her eyes to block the sun from her face. *I'm so thirsty. I'm so thirsty. Oh God...*

It had been ten days since the fishing boat capsized in a storm, taking with it the crew of eight to the bottom of the ocean. Now she wished she'd gone with them instead of having been ordered into the life raft. "What about your crew? What about you?" she'd screamed over the roar of wind and relentless waves pounding the side of the vessel. Captain Harris, a man in his late seventies with a weather-beaten face, flashed his crooked teeth. "We are men of the sea, my dear. Here we live, and here we will die."

Moments after boarding the raft, Liv watched in helpless terror as the fishing boat disappeared into the depths of the North Pacific, taking those men with it. They were fathers, sons, brothers, and husbands. She'd gotten to know each and every man during the interviews she'd conducted over her three weeks aboard as an observer, and they were good, good men. But all she could do was watch them die as she hung on for dear life, the violently rolling waves tossing her raft around like a wet sock in a drier.

Why wouldn't they come with me? Why? She'd asked herself that question over and over again. But in the days ahead, baking in the afternoon sun and shivering through the windy nights, Liv realized the captain never would have left his ship and his men would never have left him. They were a family as close knit as any, and it was the reason she'd chosen them as subjects for her dissertation. That, and

Captain Harris, who had been a friend of her father, didn't mind the intrusion.

Liv glanced at the empty plastic bottle to her side and felt her parched throat aching and burning for the water that was long gone. It had been the only provision she'd managed to grab during the storm, and not nearly enough.

You're dying, Liv. Accept it. Just let go... She'd said her tearful goodbyes this morning to her mother, father, and two sisters—Krista and Dana—when delirium had convinced her that they were real.

But, of course, they hadn't been. Her family was safe in Wrangell, Alaska, probably mourning her death along with the crew's families.

Soon they'll be right to mourn. Liv suddenly felt another bump, followed by a violent gust of wind.

Liv sat up again, but this time she saw something unexpected: land. Golden sand, black volcanic rocks jutting from the water, thick green vegetation spiked with colossal pine trees. *Sweet Jesus...*

Liv gaped at the shore, pinching her sanity. *How's this possible?* There were no landmasses for a thousand miles in any direction from the spot where the fishing boat went down. No, she wasn't a map-geek, but she wasn't a slouch in geography either. And it wasn't possible to have floated back to Alaska or any other land, for that matter.

Wait. This can't be real. It can't be. Yes, another goddamned hallucination.

She placed her hand over her empty stomach and burst with laughter. "Why not let me die?" she mumbled toward the sky, unsure of who she was speaking to.

God?

The universe?

She didn't know, and she didn't care. But to die like this wasn't fair. She was a good person who'd tried her best. Family, friends, strangers she met at the women's shelter where she volunteered—didn't matter who—she always gave what she could to everyone. Because life was all about relationships— friendship and love. It was what had drawn her to sociology for her doctorate. It was what separated humans from animals.

Liv was about to lie back again when she suddenly noticed a naked man with long black hair emerging from the waves onto the beach. Her imaginary beach.

Liv rubbed her eyes, but the island was still there.

Ohmygod. She cupped her hands over her mouth. *He's real?*

Liv started waving her arms in the air, trying to scream, but couldn't manage anything above a raspy whisper.

Oh God, please! Please turn around and look at me! Instead, the man grabbed a piece of black cloth from the sand and dried off, looking like he was about to head into the forest skirting the edge of the beach.

No, no, no. Don't go! She started to paddle, but that was when she noticed the cold water pouring in through a tear along the bottom of the raft. *What? What the hell?*

Bump.

Her body jolted once more, and then a large gray fin popped from the water.

"Oh shit!" This time the words came out loud and clear.

Suddenly, the colossal man turned in her direction. He stared for a moment and then dove head first into the waves. His muscular arms exploded from the water with each powerful stroke, pulling him closer and closer at a speed that wasn't humanly possible.

"Go back!" she tried to yell, but only produced a throaty whisper. *No, no...please turn back.*

All she could do now was hope that her salvation was a fantasy or that if he wasn't, the shark wouldn't kill him. Or her.

Two large hands popped from the water and gripped the side of the raft. If she'd had the strength to gasp, she would've. The man's face appeared just inches from hers, and it was exquisite—short black beard and dark-green eyes surrounded by long lashes. Ropes of wet black hair snaked down his deeply bronzed, powerful-looking shoulders.

"How the *fuck* did you get here, woman?" he growled while studying her, his thick lips lacking any sign of warmth or reassurance.

Of course, she didn't have the mental clarity to respond.

"Well," he said, "if you live, maybe you'll save me from the Collection—waste of fucking time."

Liv now had no doubt in her mind that she was still hallucinating. Large, beautiful men didn't paddle around in the middle of the ocean and strike up random conversations.

Bump.

The man's body jerked to one side. He winced and then glanced over his shoulder before being yanked beneath the surface.

Oh shit. Oh shit. The shark. She used her last ounce of energy to flip to her stomach. There was no sign of her manly hallucination, but red liquid clouded the water, encircling the raft. She wanted to scream, but she could barely swallow let alone make a sound.

Large bubbles surfaced next to her, and then the man's head reappeared.

He half-gasped half-growled. "Fucking shark. Bit my ankle." He swung his arm and flung a large gray mass right into her raft.

Whatthefuck? The shark flopped around, the lower half of its jaw missing and gushing blood.

Liv stared, unable to believe there was a ten-foot shark bleeding out in her raft.

"And now we've got dinner." The man smiled at her, but it was a cold, calculating sort of smile that didn't touch his eyes. "By the way, welcome to El Corazón."

CHAPTER TWO

*Rescue Hopes Abandoned for
Alaskan Fishing Boat, Nine Lost at Sea*

*Late yesterday, U.S. Coast Guard abandoned
efforts to locate survivors from the Alaskan fishing
boat* Sons of the Sea. *Coast Guard representatives
stated that the unseasonably rough waters
experienced in the North Pacific over one week ago
were caused by unusual weather patterns and likely
took the crew by surprise. Although rescue efforts
began immediately, no survivors or traces of the
vessel have been found. Aboard were 29-yr-old
Olivia Stratton, who had been observing the crew
as part of her sociology dissertation, and John
Harris, the captain and owner of the vessel, along
with seven other crew members, whose names have
not yet been released.*

From behind the antique desk in his twentieth-floor corner office situated in downtown Seattle, Roen Doran glanced at the picture of the woman mentioned in the newspaper article. "Too bad. She was pretty." Hypnotic dark eyes surrounded by thick lashes, full lips, and high cheekbones.

An even greater shame, however, was the cargo vessel bound for Shanghai he'd lost in that same storm. A one-hundred-million-dollar, state-of-the-art ship gone. Frankly, he didn't fucking buy it. Ships didn't disappear like that. Oil slicks, debris, human remains—something would've floated to the surface. Maybe if the goddamned Coast Guard hadn't been so damned busy looking for that piece of shit fishing boat, they might've found his ship. Right now it was probably docked somewhere in Indonesia, its ten-million-dollar cargo being sold on the black market. And the crew of thirty-five? Likely executed.

It was the first time one of his ships had been pirated. *And it will be the fucking last.* Not only would he double up on armed escorts through international waters, but he would find those SOBs and have their asses hauled off to some fuck-hole of a third world country where bribes were welcomed. He'd pay to have those men beaten and hanged as a message to anyone else who might think his ships were an easy target.

Suddenly, a familiar wave of sharp pinpricks washed over him and his chest tightened. It wasn't a heart attack—at thirty-four, he was far too young and far too healthy for that—but it goddamned felt like one and had been going on for weeks. "It's probably stress, Roen. When's the last time you took a vacation?" his doctor had asked a few days ago after Roen finally broke down and went for a visit. Roen had told the SOB to mind his own damned business. "Just send my blood-work results to my assistant." Everything had come back clean. Just as he thought. So what was really the matter with him?

Roen threw down the copy of *The Times* on his desk atop the other papers he read each day to keep current.

Goddammit. I can't breathe. Loosening his black tie, he stood and walked over to the large window overlooking the shimmering evening cityscape of glass and steel. Whatever this thing was, it felt like his own personal pestilence. He couldn't even get his dick hard this morning with...whateverthehell her name was that he'd brought home last night. Or had she brought him home because he was too pissed on scotch?

Doesn't fucking matter.

Maybe it was time to take a break. He hadn't taken a day off in ten years.

There was a faint, very recognizable knock on his door.

"What is it, Cherie?"

The petite Asian woman entered, quietly closing the door behind her. "Sir," she said, holding out a sealed white envelope marked "personal" along with a stack of papers, "I know you asked not to be bothered, but I'm leaving for the day, and this just came for you. It's from your lawyer in Chicago."

His lawyer? Phil usually called or emailed when something came up. And something always came up. With the largest fleet of cargo vessels in the world and one hundred thousand employees operating in over one hundred twenty countries, there was always something happening. Usually bad somethings—customs issues, port strikes, union negotiations. But that was why Doran Cargo was the biggest, pulling in over ten billion in revenue each year. They knew what the hell they were doing, and Roen didn't take shit from anyone. *Pirates included.*

Roen picked up the Gripmaster from his desk and began squeezing the large spring in his hand. "Put the envelope there." He glanced at the correspondence tray. "And get my asshole lawyer on the phone. Tell him it's urgent." Phil, his lawyer, knew Roen hated surprises.

Cherie dipped her head of silky black hair. "Yes, sir. Right away."

She disappeared out the door while Roen squeezed away, trying to release some tension. Wasn't working.

Moments later, the phone on his desk rang, and he hit the speaker. "What the hell is inside the envelope?"

"Oh, if it isn't the Sexiest Man of the Year," Phil said dryly.

"Stop giving me shit." That PR nightmare happened over six months ago, but Phil still brought it up. Roen wasn't sexy, he was a bastard. And he had little interest in being a celebrity. But at the time, he needed to soften his image in order to get a new merger to slide through. It worked, but the price was far beyond anything he could've imagined. Fan clubs, paparazzi, and…fucking Phil. "What's in the damned envelope?"

"I'll stop giving you shit when you stop pulling me out of meetings and saying it's an emergency when it's not."

"I said it was urgent, not an emergency. You picked up the phone. Now answer the damned question," he said coldly.

"You're really asking what's in the envelope sitting right in front of you?"

Damned lawyers. Always have to make everything into an argument. Of course, that was why he liked Phil. The bastard had no soul and his heart was made from a money clip. Just. Like. Him.

"Yes," Roen replied. "If you want to keep your million-dollar retainer, you'll tell me before I hang the hell up."

There was a grumble, but Roen knew Phil would answer the question. That was how all of Roen's relationships worked: Roen asked. People did.

"Look, Ro"—Roen stopped pumping the spring in his hand. Phil only used his nickname when the shit was about to hit—"I get paid to handle your business affairs not your personal bullshit. Otherwise, I would've called. I forwarded the paperwork to you as a courtesy because you're a friend."

"I don't have friends. What's in the envelope, Phil? Last time," Roen growled. Was it a paternity suit from one of the women he'd fucked? He was always careful, but one thing he'd learned, some of these women went out of their way to create accidents.

"Your father's will."

Roen sat down in his black leather chair. "Will?" His father was dead?

"No one told you," Phil realized. "Sorry. I assumed you knew—the paperwork showed up from his lawyers. I thought you'd been notified."

Good riddance. Roen was sixteen when he'd said goodbye to that prick, and he'd meant it.

"I didn't know," Roen said, rubbing his brow, "but it doesn't matter. The man was a..." He was about to say a disgrace, an embarrassment, a psychotic lunatic who'd put Roen, his mother, and younger brother through the worst possible torment with his paranoid delusions and environmental crusades that included terrorist-like activities. It was the reason their mother fled Glasgow, along with him and his brother, to the States when he was ten, where they lived under assumed names. His mother did everything in her power to hide them, even making them speak "American" so people were less likely to notice them. But despite her efforts, it wouldn't take long for their father to find them. He always found them. Then they'd run again. After a few years of trying, his mother eventually gave up. Perhaps that was the beginning of the end for her.

"Never mind," Roen said, deciding not to waste his time thinking about any of that. "Go back to your meeting."

"I plan to. And I'm shutting off my cell."

"Do whatever the hell you like. But if you're not available when I need you, I'll find someone who is."

"You're a sadistic prick, Roen."

"Yes. And I'm not losing any sleep over it."

"That's because you can't lose what you don't have." Phil referred to the fact that Roen didn't sleep. He worked all hours of the day and expected the people who worked for him to be available. Period. Lucky for Phil, though, Roen trusted him and that gave the man a degree of latitude when it came to their relationship.

"I run a shipping company. It never sleeps, so neither do I." Two hours each day would do it.

"Yes, but you have capable, well-paid people who can run the company for you. Not to mention you also have a new, hot piece of ass in your bed every night. Yet, you still choose to work. By the way, is it true you fucked that actress last week and then asked her to leave at two in the morning because you had a conference call?"

It was true. But the call had been pertaining to an important deal in Shanghai, and he hadn't wanted any distractions. Now, why had she felt the need to tell the tabloids? It was foolish to believe he gave a crap about what anyone thought.

"Women come and go," Roen said, sidestepping the question about the actress, "but my company took fifteen years to build." And fact was, beautiful women were a cheap commodity. All Roen had to do was walk into a room and they flocked. "There's something about you," they'd say. Or, "Your eyes are such an unusual shade of green."

Truth was, he didn't really know why women seemed uninhibited in his presence or aggressively pursued him like hungry animals. Maybe it was a combination of his money and six-six height or his thick light brown hair—hell, who cared?

Roen's eyes gravitated toward the unopened envelope. "Goodbye, Phil."

"Wait. Since I have you on the phone, I sent those insurance claims. Make sure you sign them toda—"

Roen hung up. He wasn't in the mood to talk business now that the envelope had taken on a whole new meaning. It was an official end to a relationship he didn't want. He only hoped that inside would be vindication—an apology from his father for the pain he'd caused Roen's now deceased mother and brother. That man had taken away the only two people Roen had ever loved because of his crazed bullshit.

Roen opened the envelope and found a letter paper-clipped to an old map that looked straight out of a ridiculous Looney Tunes episode—a few landmarks and a giant "X" right in the middle of the page. He skimmed the letter—some random garble about an island in the North Pacific. Clearly, his father had been a crazy asshole right until the bitter end. *Case in point...*

Roen, my boy, this island and its treasures will become yours if you choose to claim it. And I hope you do because there is no greater cause on this earth than protecting it. However, you must always remember, whatever you do, to never turn your back on that which the island asks of you. Never question the island, son, because—

Roen chucked the letter into the wastepaper basket along with the map. He wanted nothing to do with it or his father. *Leave the past where it belongs.*

He picked up the stack of insurance papers and began skimming through them before signing. Page after page of affidavits, cargo valuations, waivers, and…

"What the hell?" The report filed by the Coast Guard showed the approximate location of where they believed the cargo vessel went down.

He dug his father's map from the trash. There were no lines of longitude or latitude, but the position was the same: approximately two thousand miles west of San Francisco and a thousand miles south of the Delarof Islands, the most southern point of Alaska.

Roen dialed Cherie. He knew she wouldn't really go home until he told her to leave because she doted on him like a lovesick puppy. No, he'd never laid a finger on the woman and never would. She was under his employ and that meant something to him. Even selfish pricks needed to draw the line somewhere.

"Yes, sir?"

"What ships do we have on the Seattle to Shanghai route?"

"One moment." Cherie clicked away on her keyboard. "You've got one ship departing Chinese waters now and an empty vessel unloading at port."

"Here in Seattle?"

"Yes," she replied.

"Tell the crew I'm sailing with them."

"Uh…okay. Is everything all right, sir?" It was highly unusual for Roen to ever step foot on a ship, and that was because the motion made him violently ill. Ironic, given his fascination with boats, but maybe it was his disdain for the sea that drove his need to conquer it. He wasn't sure, nor did he care. Just as long as he didn't have to go swimming. Or touch any fish. Fish were vile.

"Everything's fine," he replied. "Just cancel my meetings the rest of the week. If anything urgent comes up, send it to Orman." Dylan Orman was president of operations and his right-hand man for the last decade. Orman could handle most anything in a pinch.

"Yes, sir. I'll do it right away," Cherie said.

"Good. And make sure there's a helicopter onboard." Every ship had a landing pad for emergencies, but rarely carried air transport. They'd definitely be needing one if he was going to find the exact spot on the map.

He hung up the phone and suddenly felt that dark cloud washing over him again. His heart pounded like a goddamned war drum and his gut twisted into excruciating knots. *What the hell is wrong with me?*

CHAPTER THREE

Lying on a hard floor, her body screaming with pain, Liv awoke on her back and stared up at a beamed ceiling. *Dear God, where am I?*

She lifted her head slowly. The room, with quaint French windows, reminded her of a beach bungalow she'd once stayed at. Only, this home, whoever it belonged to, was sparsely decorated. No pictures on the light-gray, wood-paneled walls. No light fixtures, either. Just two hand-carved chairs and a small wooden table in the corner.

Water, I need water, she thought, once again feeling herself drift out of consciousness, the room beginning to fade to black. She knew she only had minutes left if she wanted to live. Her heart rate was rapid, her body shivered, and every muscle spasmed. *Maybe you're dead already.* Of course, she'd thought the same this morning when a strange man tore part of a shark's head off and then towed her raft to shore like some bizarre dream.

Oh, God. I'm so thirsty. Why hadn't the man given her water? That question was more important than any of the others, but dying did that to a person—made everything else feel trivial. Where she was or how that man had managed to slay a shark with his bare hands were questions that would only matter if she lived.

The front door swung open, and sunlight poured inside from behind the tall, strong silhouette of a nearly naked man.

"Why's she covered in blood?" said another man with a deep, authoritative voice, from somewhere outside.

"I killed a shark. It got messy." The man standing in the doorway shrugged. "But you'd better decide about her quickly."

"Do *not* push me, Shane," said the man outside.

Shane. The guy in the doorway is Shane, she thought.

Shane shook his head. "I merely meant to point out that she's almost dead."

"I can see that, asshole. But what I cannot understand is how she got here."

"She was sent to me by the ocean," Shane said, "which is why I wish to keep her; she is a gift."

There was a long moment of silence. "Right you are. She is a gift, but who says this pretty package was meant for you?"

"But—"

"Did she come labeled with your name?" the man outside asked.

"No," said Shane.

"Then you will give her sacred water, and she will be put up for claiming. Tonight."

There was a low growl from Shane. "She's not worth dying for. Look at her."

"Then that's your choice. But say another word, Shane, and you'll be spending the night with the maids."

Maids. Do they have butlers, too?

Liv heard heavy steps crushing rocks and dirt as the man walked away. Moments later, Shane kneeled over her, holding something in his hands. "What a fucking asshole," he grumbled. "All right, sweetheart, drink up." He lifted her head and held a leather pouch with a spout to her lips.

The water touched her tongue, and she'd never tasted anything so delicious—better than any chocolate or pastry. Better than any kiss she'd ever experienced.

She opened her mouth and swallowed. The liquid coated her dry, burning throat as it went down. She grabbed his hand and held on, vigorously sucking the life-giving water.

"That's right," he said, "drink up." But the way he said it sounded angry, like he wanted her to choke on it. She couldn't imagine why, but she didn't care. The damned water tasted so good.

Within seconds of the water entering her mouth, she felt an odd sensation as her body absorbed the fluid. Her vision immediately cleared, and her mind right along with it.

Holy crap. People didn't recover that quickly from dehydration. Then again, what did she know?

She was half out of her mind, and there were no events in her life she could compare to.

When the water ran out, she looked up at the man, now seeing him clearly. His deep green eyes shimmered with the sunlight pouring in through the open doorway. His beard was short enough that she could see the angular contours of his twenty-something face, and his long, black hair hung in unkempt ropes as though it hadn't been brushed in a very long while.

He smiled and displayed a perfect set of white teeth. "Better?"

"More," she said, relieved to hear the sound of her own voice again—clear and smooth, not rough and scratchy from lack of moisture.

"That was enough to keep you from dying." He stood and headed for the door. "Not that it matters now since I don't get to have you," he grumbled under his breath. "I'll be back in a while to check on you. And if you value your life, you won't leave this dwelling."

Liv's brain tried to process Shane's words, but her body felt overwhelmed with a burst of tingles and heat.

She looked at her cracked, blistered hands. The skin began healing right in front of her eyes. *What in the…?*

"Wait!" she yelled at the brawny, shirtless man closing the door. "What did you give me?"

He stopped and shot her a look. "Water," he said with a voice so frigid that she knew he didn't welcome her question, nor would he be providing further details. But it was more than water. She'd just watched her body spontaneously heal.

"Can you at least tell me where I am?"

He flashed a sinister grin. "I already told you, on the island of El Corazón."

"Where is that?" She'd never heard of it.

"It's the center of the ocean, the center of everything."

That made no sense. In fact, it sounded downright creepy. "Do you have a phone? I need to call my family and tell them I'm okay."

He stared at her as if she were the daftest person on the planet.

Oh, God. The two men had just talked about keeping her. Yes, now that her mind cleared, they'd said they were going to put her up for something they called "claiming."

"You're not going to let me leave here, are you?" she asked, having already realized the truth.

He laughed. "There is only one way off this island—for a woman, that is. As you'll see soon enough."

Oh, Jesus. She assumed he meant a body bag or stuffed into a drum or some other hideous form of body disposal. Of course, that would come after they did stuff to her—that's what this "claiming" had to be.

"Just so you know, I'd slit my own throat before I'd let anyone rape me," she said evenly, meaning every word. Liv volunteered at a battered women's shelter near her apartment in Seattle—where she attended college and lived during the school year.

The work had started out as a three-week commitment as part of a class assignment related to a women's issues course. But three weeks became four and then five and then a year. It wasn't always easy finding time to volunteer, while holding down a part-time job as a professor's assistant and working on her PhD, but from day one, Liv couldn't turn her back on those women. They came to that old brick building near the marina broken, desperate, and looking for salvation. The brutality of men was something Liv would never understand. And with every face she saw—some with small children in tow—and every hand she held, Liv began hating the men who preyed on women. With every fiber of her being. It was an unspeakable atrocity to use a woman's love against her like that, distorting it into some sort of psychological noose. She'd rather die than let one of those disgusting excuses for a man touch her.

Shane raised a brow and grinned sadistically. "In the island's five thousand years of recorded history, not one woman has ever been forced. They always give willingly. You'll be no different once you've been claimed."

Does he think I'm an idiot? Whoever these men were, they had no intention of treating her like a human being.

Shane grabbed the handle to close the door. "Like I said; if you value your life, you'll stay here until I come for you."

"If I don't?" she asked to test him.

He flashed an ominous smile over his bronzed bare shoulder. "We have all sorts of monsters on this island. You wouldn't want to make one angry."

He closed the door behind him, and Liv hopped from the floor, scrambling to the window to watch him disappear into the thick vegetation of the forest.

She looked down at her now perfectly healed feet, running the men's conversation through her head. She would be put up for some kind of grabs they'd called a "claiming" tonight. No, she had no fucking clue where she was or where she'd go, but sitting in this cabin, waiting for them to return was stupid. Whatever "monsters" were out there would be better than facing the monsters who'd "rescued" her. Then there was the fact that he'd ripped the jaw off of a shark. A shark. Ten feet long.

Her head whipped around, and she headed for the doorway that led to a small kitchen with shelves on one wall opposite a grimy fireplace. Another small table occupied the center of the room, and on it, she found a small cloth sack with a cinch next to a bowl of apples. She grabbed some fruit and stuffed them inside the bag. On the wooden shelves, she saw bunches of dried herbs—tea perhaps— bottles of what smelled like rum, some preserves, a few mugs and...

She picked up a clear bottle and gave it a sniff. *Odorless.* Was this that stuff Shane had given her? Because having more of it probably wasn't a good idea. On the other hand, if she found nothing else, she might be forced to drink it anyway. She placed it in the little sack and tied the cinch around her wrist.

She then charged back out to the living room and upstairs, where she found a small bedroom with a hammock in the corner and a few narrow shelves just opposite. A copy of *The Complete Psychological Works of Sigmund Freud* lay next to a stack of black linen cloths.

Okay. That's strange. What would he be doing with that book? Liv grabbed one of the cloths and held it up, realizing this was what Shane wore around his waist. Other than that, she found nothing. Not even a bathroom. He lived like a man from the 1800s—nothing modern, everything made by hand.

She grabbed two of the cloths and tied one around each foot in lieu of shoes before bolting downstairs and out the back door of the kitchen. Sprinting for her life into the forest and following the distant sound of waves, Liv ducked sharp branches and weaved through thorny bushes. The forest reminded her of home with the crisp pine-scented air and dense, hardy foliage. Her home was also an island, but they had snowcapped mountains, bears, and salmon, not gargantuan psychopaths.

After ten minutes of dodging trees and pushing her body through wall after wall of brush, she realized she didn't feel winded. Not one little bit. Whatever that man had given her wasn't like any narcotic or vitamin she'd ever heard of. Frankly, if she wasn't already scared as hell, she'd be freaking the hell out about having some foreign substance in her body.

When she finally reached the black and gold-sanded shore, she halted in shock. The entire sky shimmered and sparkled with hues of flaming orange. It was magnificent but frightening, because skies like that only existed in dreams.

Yeah, but this isn't a dream. You need to find a way off this island. A small boat. A phone...something.

Looking side to side, trying to figure out which way to run, someone sacked her from behind, and she fell into the sand.

"I warned you, landlover!" It was that Shane guy.

He picked her up and twisted her around to face him. "This time, I'm going to tie you—"

Liv thrust her knee into his groin and the man instantly released her, groaning in agony. She ran as fast as she could, trying to stick to the wetter, firmer sand, hoping she could make it just around the bend ahead, where she might have a chance of cutting inland and hiding.

Run, Liv. Run hard. You're almost—

"You stupid bitch!" Shane pushed her from behind, and her entire body flew into the shallow waves. He grabbed the back of her neck and shoved her face down, holding her under the sandy, turbulent water.

Oh God. Oh God. He's trying to kill me. She clawed at his hands and kicked as hard as she could, but he was so strong. Just when she felt her panicked, out-of-breath body demanding air—air that wasn't there—Shane pulled her up.

She sucked in a breath and screamed, "Help! Somebody!"

"I'll help you, you cunt," Shane bellowed with sadistic joy. "Now take a big breath because it might be your last."

"No!" she yelled.

Shane gripped her by a fistful of hair and pushed her under again. She twisted and clawed for her life, thinking for sure this was it and feeling angry as hell that her life would end like this. It wasn't fair to make it so far, only to die at the hands of some asshole.

Unexpectedly, Shane let her up. "Lucky for you, your fate's already been decided." Then he dragged her from the water and threw her over his shoulder so quickly it nearly gave her whiplash.

But as Shane turned to head back toward his cabin, she heard him grunt and they both tipped over into the sand.

Liv scrambled to get Shane off of her leg, and that's when she saw him. The man was absolutely stunning. Like a sex god ripped straight from the pages of Greek mythology, with gloriously thick, golden-streaked, caramel-brown hair cut just above the ears and a menacingly tall, powerful frame. The exquisite angles on his lightly stubbled face were chiseled male perfection—strong jaw, supple lips, cleft chin, and perfectly shaped toffee-brown eyebrows.

Liv felt a jolt in her chest. "Who are you?" she asked, unable to speak with the full volume of her voice. And why was this real-life god standing on the beach in black slacks and a white dress shirt, dripping wet?

He tossed the thick branch he held in his hand and then dipped his head, narrowing his exotic green eyes, studying her. "I'm Roen Doran. How the hell did you end up on this island, Olivia Stratton?"

CHAPTER FOUR

"How do you know me?" Panting hard from the adrenaline, Liv got to her feet, unsure if she should be running from this beautiful man or running toward him. Something about this Roen Doran felt menacing.

"Your picture was all over the papers. I lost millions of fucking dollars because of you," he said with a tiny hint of an accent. What was it? English?

She blinked at him. "I-I don't understand."

"Neverthehellmind. What are you doing here? And who the hell is *that*?" His gaze flashed to an unconscious Shane lying in the sand with his bare ass on display.

Dripping wet, she shook her head, trying to catch her breath. "I don't know. My life raft drifted here, and he fished me from the waves."

"It looked like he was trying to put you back. What did you do to piss him off?"

Why would he assume she'd done anything wrong?

"I ran from him," she replied, "because one of them—their leader, I think—said he's going to sell me or put me up for auction or something."

Roen Doran rubbed his brows, wincing in pain. What was the matter with him?

"Great, just what I need," he mumbled. "How many are there?"

Wow. What compassion.

"I don't know. I only heard two men's voices, but from the way they spoke, there are more."

Roen looked down at his wet black leather shoes. "I don't have time for this crap," he said to himself and then reached into his pocket and pulled out a phone. He stared at it for a moment and then held it to the sky. "No signal. We'll need to wait until a satellite passes over." He then bent his large, well-muscled frame and slipped his feet from his wet socks and shoes.

The man's toes were perfectly pedicured. The most perfect set of man-toes she'd ever seen. Which, despite his civilized attire, seemed odd given how masculine he looked—like the kind of guy who'd sooner punch someone in the face rather than let them touch his toes.

"Can you walk?" he asked.

"Yes. But where are we going?" Not that she cared. Anywhere away from Shane was good, even if this guy seemed like a callous jerk.

"To find a place to wait until help arrives. Hopefully, they're on the way already."

"Who?"

"The crew of my ship. They're only a few miles away, and by now they've realized my helicopter went down."

That's when Liv realized why Roen seemed familiar. "Wait. You're Roen Doran."

"I said that already." He turned his body toward the water and began walking incredibly fast with those big long legs of his. "We need to step on the wet sand so the waves wash away our tracks."

Liv followed closely behind. "I didn't realize you were *that* Roen Doran." The man's name was synonymous with shipping, and he was perhaps the most sought-after billionaire bachelor on the planet. He'd even earned the Sexiest Man of the Year cover. He was also known for being a womanizer, cutthroat businessman, and a bit of a recluse. Yes, she may have read a few articles about him, but out of sheer curiosity only. She wasn't one of *those* women—the thousands who worshipped him like a god, dedicating websites, blogs and entire Facebook pages to him.

He continued at a fast pace, and Liv glanced over her shoulder, checking to be sure that Shane was still out. Thankfully, he was.

"So what are you doing here?" she asked.

"I was looking for—I don't know—I was looking for something," he said in that deep, hypnotically masculine voice.

"You were out in the middle of the ocean, looking for something, but you don't know what it was?" She found that strange.

"It's a long story, and one I don't care to discuss."

Okay... "What happened to your helicopter?" she asked.

"The island *foking* appeared out of nowhere, and we clipped the tail of our helicopter on some cliffs."

Foking?

"Who's we?" she asked.

"My pilot. He's dead."

Roen didn't seem to care one little bit.

"I'm sorry to hear that," Liv said. "But thank God you're alive. You saved me."

"I haven't saved you yet. And frankly, it's not a priority."

Jesus. Could this man possibly be any more heartless? "You're serious."

"Now that I found this place, I want answers, and I'm not leaving until I get them." He marched along the shallow waves, unconcerned with her in any way. And it wasn't like the man didn't know she'd been lost at sea for ten days. He knew damned well who she was.

"But I have to get off this—"

"I wasn't the idiot who decided to do my homework on a fishing boat in the middle of the Pacific."

She scoffed. "Excuse me, but it was my dissertation. And where the hell do you get off talking to me like that?"

"Like what?"

Like you're a complete asshole lacking any compassion for what I've just been through. "Never mind." Having a discussion about his shortcomings as a human being wasn't going to help her.

He held up his phone again, pointing it toward the sky. "Piece of bloody crap cost me five thousand dollars and doesn't work. That salesman just lost his job."

He'd spent five thousand on a phone? Did it produce water? Because despite feeling better, she was still thirsty. "I need something to drink."

He looked at her. "Sorry. Fresh out of martinis."

Wow. Just...wow. Yes, the man was drop-dead gorgeous and too beautiful for words—and every bit the vision of brutal masculinity women praised him for being—but the man truly was a colossal ass-hat.

"No. You don't understand," she said. "I'm *really* thirsty."

"You look fine to me." He focused on his phone, pressing buttons and swiping the screen.

"Look!" She grabbed his arm, squeezing hard and shocked as hell by what she found. A rock-solid forearm without an ounce of squishiness. "I've had *maybe* a glass of water in the last five days and that includes whatever crack-infused crap that psycho Neanderthal just fed me to bring me back from the dead."

He glanced at her with a sneer as if to say it wasn't his problem.

Okay. Screw being nice. "I know that underneath the deceivingly handsome face, which allows you to pass for a real human being, is a complete narcissistic asshole, but I'm begging you. I don't know what he made me drink, but I know I'm going to die if I don't have water."

He turned his entire body toward her and looked down, making her feel extremely small. "What do I get in return?" he asked with that deep, deep overtly sinful voice that one might easily find addictive.

Liv's mouth fell open. "You can't be serious."

"Nothing is free." His exotic green eyes twinkled with a roguish glint and his lips—full enough to make them look sensual even when he wasn't trying—twitched with a smile. "And you know how us narcissistic assholes can be. Especially after surviving helicopter crashes and saving strange women from defilement. Personally, it puts me in one hell of a greedy mood." His eyes momentarily flashed to her chest. Then again.

"Did you just look at my breasts?"

"Your T-shirt is wet. I couldn't help it," he said unapologetically.

Liv glanced down at her chest. *Yep. The man can see everything, right down to my perky pink— ohmygod. Wait.*

Liv pointed a finger at him. "You weren't just suggesting I pay you by—"

He held out his large hand, and his full lips dropped any hint of a smile. "I don't know what you've read or think you know about me, but I assure you, the exploitation of distressed women is not on my list of pursuits."

The man's tone sounded genuinely offended, and his fierce gaze offered the exclamation point.

Liv blew out a breath. Okay. They were both in a not-so-great situation. And he had definitely helped her earlier. "I'm sorry. I was out of line. And I'm really truly grateful you helped me, but I don't think I'll make it much longer without some fluids. All I'm asking for is a little help—"

Liv felt her knees buckle under the weight of her dehydrated body.

Strong arms caught her before she hit the wet sand. "For *foke's* sake, woman."

She looked up into those deep green eyes with hazel rings around the pupils gazing down on her with disgust.

"Why?" she mumbled.

"Why, what?" he snarled.

"Why do you hate women?"

"I don't hate women. I hate weakness."

"I'm not weak. I'm just thirsty," she grumbled.

He stared for a long moment, intensely studying her eyes, her lips, her every facial detail. And when their eyes met again, she felt an odd sensation pass through her, like a jolt of electricity. The moment didn't last longer than half a breath, and in a million years she'd never be able to fully articulate what she felt, but gazing into his eyes was like swimming in an ocean filled with torment, rage, sadness, and…well, it was how she felt when she'd been in that raft.

More importantly, however, she saw—or sensed, really—something else in the depths of those piercing green eyes. Whatever it was made her heart tingle and told her that this man wasn't the coldhearted person he pretended to be. Because a person without any heart couldn't possibly provoke such deep emotion inside her. It was impossible.

"You don't scare me, Mr. Doran. So stop being an ass and find some water."

He laughed and then the corners of those lips pulled into a breathtaking smile "All right, Miss Stratton. But don't think I'm going to be your nursemaid. You'll have to take care of yourself. At least until my ship sends a search party."

"Liv. Call me Liv," she mumbled quietly and blacked out.

ॐ∙ॐ

What the hell have I gotten myself into? Roen grumbled to himself, holding the overly thin, dripping wet brunette, who looked surprisingly sinful in her dirty, tattered clothes—khaki pants ripped into shorts and a white T-shirt with the sleeves torn off. She also had a thick layer of grime stuck to her face, and was that... He dipped his head and took a whiff. *She smells like chum.*

He then noticed dried blood splatters on her clothes. *What did they do to her?*

He carried her across the narrow beach to the tree line and gently set her down in the shade on a patch of damp leaves. He rolled her onto her side, where the bloodstains seemed more concentrated, and inspected her back. She had a long lean frame with nice curves, but it was obvious she hadn't eaten in a while. Her rib cage showed through and her arms looked pencil thin. Luckily, however, he didn't see any wounds. On that side anyway.

He rolled her onto her back and gripped the front of her wet shirt, pausing for a moment. Touching her was unexpectedly turning him on. No doubt the woman was beautiful—probably a knockout when cleaned up and fed—however, this was no time to be thinking with his dick.

Be a man and get over it. You've seen plenty of beautiful naked women. He lifted the front of her shirt and tried not to notice her large, plump breasts packed tightly into a sheer pink bra, her pink nipples showing through. *All right. So what? The woman has perfect natural breasts, but those aren't for you.* Of course, that didn't mean he was going to forget them anytime soon or hadn't thoroughly enjoyed the view.

"Well"—his words stuck in his throat—"you seem to be injury free on the front side, too." He quickly inspected the back and sides of her head. It was difficult to tell with so much hair—wet, long, and sticky with salt water—but he saw no sign of injury there either. The blood hadn't come from her; however, he had no doubt the man he'd hit with a branch intended to harm her.

Sick bastard. Roen lowered Liv's shirt, trying to figure out what he would do next. He'd meant what he'd said about her situation not being a priority, but that was because he wasn't in much better shape than his new "companion." He just happened to hide it well. Fact was, whatever was wrong with him only seemed to be getting worse. And now he was on the brink of losing his fucking mind, including having just seen his dead mother.

Wait right there. That was not your mother. You watched her body go into the ground. Yet, the moment right before the helicopter's tail slammed into the cliff—a cliff that literally came out of nowhere—he saw her standing at its edge, waving him back, telling him not to come here. Within the blink of an eye, she was gone and the helicopter spun out of control, hurtling toward the waves below. At the moment of impact, a chunk of windshield went right through the pilot, but Roen was ejected as the doors blasted open. He was damned lucky not to have been strapped in or chopped up by the blades.

The question still begged, however, why the hell had he seen his mother? It was as if this dark cloud of his wanted to make him think of the past he'd fought so hard to forget.

"Get a bloody grip, Roen." He shook his head and picked up Liv again.

Her brown eyes fluttered open. "I don't want to die," she mumbled deliriously. "Dana needs me to help with the party."

Roen didn't know who this Dana was, but obviously, Liv was not lucid.

"Krista won't help," Liv continued muttering. "She's with the penguins..."

Roen raised a brow. *All right, then. Parties and penguins.*

"I can't die. I can't," she said.

Each time he glanced down at the beautiful mumbling woman in his arms, his eyes lingered just a bit longer. Something about looking at her felt... goddamned euphoric, actually. Honestly, it was something he found hard to explain.

"You're not going to die, but where did the blood come from?" he asked.

"There's a shark in my raft. I don't want to die."

Roen was about to ask what shark, but in that moment, he was hit with yet another vision of his mother. It was of his last moments with her in the hospital when he was seventeen. The social worker told him she would be fine after the operation to repair her heart, but his mother—dazed from the medication—kept telling him that she didn't want to die and to take care of his younger brother, Lyle. "Tell him to stay away from the water."

"I don't understand," he'd said, trying to hold himself together.

"Yes! You do understand," she'd said, her golden brown hair matted with sweat and her brown eyes surrounded by burst blood vessels. "Promise me, Roen. Promise you'll keep him away. You have to stay away, too. Don't go anywhere near the ocean. They're coming for you."

When Roen had asked who, his mother lost consciousness. They would never speak again. And tragically, Lyle would die in the ocean two years later. From that day on, Roen hated the damned ocean, but he refused to fear it. No. He'd conquer the damned thing.

"I need to see my family again," Liv muttered. "I'm giving a speech at the party..." Her voice faded away and she was out again.

"You're going to be fine. I'll make sure of it." And strangely, he meant it, which shocked the hell out of him. It simply wasn't like him to care about anyone but himself. *This place must be messing with my head.*

Regardless, Roen had always been a man of his word, so he'd do his best to help her. He didn't know where they were going, but from the slope of the steep snowcapped peak at the center of the island, he guessed any water would be at its base.

After one hour of hiking with Liv in his arms, Roen found what he'd hoped: a small swimming hole filled by a trickling stream. Unfortunately, the water looked like an undrinkable, murky green mess.

Well, at least I got a workout. Out of breath, Roen set Liv down, propping her back against a large pine tree. He bent over, blowing out an exhausted breath. *Bloody hell.* Now he was thirsty, too. And he wasn't a damned boy scout, but he knew enough not to drink standing water that wasn't boiled. The stream flowing in didn't have enough current to assume the water was any cleaner.

He glanced up at the sharp rocky peak, reminiscent of a dormant volcano, jutting into the bright orange sky. *A damned weird sunset for a damned weird island.*

In any case, he could hike all the way up to the source of the water, but that was a few thousand feet and nightfall was approaching fast.

He looked down at Liv's peaceful face and noticed how her long, dark eyelashes fanned out and her lips naturally puckered as if she were begging for a kiss.

Did you just hear yourself, man? Begging for a kiss? What the bloody foke is wrong with you? Stop looking at the woman.

Roen also noticed Liv had a little burlap sack tied around her wrist and her hand had turned ghostly white. The thing was probably cutting off her circulation.

He removed the small bag and looked inside, finding a few apples and a bottle of liquid that appeared to be water. Curious, he removed the cork and gave it a quick whiff before tasting it with the tip of his tongue. The flavor was purer than any spring water. He swallowed the few drops in his mouth and instantly felt a pleasant burning sensation in his gut like fine tequila.

What the hell is this stuff? he thought to himself while taking a deep breath, savoring the euphoric rush unlike any high he'd ever encountered. Not pot—like he'd tried in college and put him to sleep. Not like cumming that made him forget who he was for a few lousy seconds. Not like the rush of acquiring a competitor in a hostile takeover. No, he'd never felt a rush like this.

He glanced down at his arm, watching as the muscle seemed to fill out, stretching against the fabric of his long-sleeve shirt. *What the bloody f...?* And in that moment, the painful tightening in his chest lifted, that invisible dark cloud dissolved, and he could breathe again.

Liv wasn't lying. She'd mentioned they'd given her some sort of drug-laced water, but he'd thought she was merely exaggerating as women often do.

Not this time. He stared at the bottle, entirely unafraid but unable to come to grips with whatever was inside—some sort of miracle drug.

Perhaps this was the real reason his father wanted him to find the island: Compensation for the lifetime of pain he'd inflicted. But then, why did the crazy bastard say this had to be hidden from the world?

He was probably too damned insane to understand the value. Or he was too frightened that someone would try to take it away. But Roen wasn't afraid. *I know exactly how to protect what's mine.*

His eyes gravitated toward Liv's beautiful face— those pouty, sensual lips, those high cheekbones, that perfectly straight, perky nose. The fact that she had dirt smudged all over her face yet still looked so sinfully sexy was a testament to her natural beauty. Every time he looked at her, he became more convinced that she might actually be the most stunning woman he'd ever seen, which, frankly, said a hell of a lot.

"Roen?" Liv's eyes cracked open.

He quickly looked away and slid his phone from his pocket. *Stop ogling the woman. What the hell is the matter with me?*

"Roen?" she repeated.

Ignoring her, he held up the phone and noticed a small signal. "There we go…" He punched in a number and held it to his ear. The thing rang, but heavy static filled the line, and then the signal dropped. "Sonofabitch." He again raised the device, but it was no good.

"Please. I'm so thirsty."

He glanced down at her face with wide dark eyes sunken from thirst. She looked like an angel who'd fallen from the skies, begging for her life.

Stop. You won't help anyone if you start feeling bad for her. Compassion made people vulnerable. It made them weak.

She reached out to the pool of water to her side.

"It might have parasites," he said, "which in your weakened state would kill you."

"I don't care. I need water."

Roen slipped the small bottle from his pocket. "This is the only water we've got, but it's…" He paused, unsure how to describe it, frankly. "It's that water you were telling me about."

She shook her head. "Then I don't want it. I'd rather take my chances with the amoebas."

"The way I see it, you don't have a choice; you're too weak to crawl over to that cesspool on your own, and I'm not carrying you. So it's this or nothing." He removed the small cork and crouched, holding the bottle to her lips. "Drink."

She looked away, but opened her mouth. He could see she didn't like being pushed around, and he couldn't blame her. He hated it, too.

She gulped the entire contents, and right before his eyes, he watched a bit of color return to her face. Whatever was in that water was powerful.

She sighed and rested her head back on the dirt. "It's not enough. I need more."

"I don't have more."

"Give me that." Her eyes focused on the pool.

"It's not—"

"It's not your fucking choice," she said. "You're not the one dying, Roen Doran."

"Yes. That is correct. However…" He stopped himself mid-thought. He'd been about to say that she was his, but that was ludicrous. She wasn't *his* anything because they'd only just met. He'd agreed to help her find water, and that was all. *That's right. Stop thinking with your cock, Roen.*

"If that's what you want," he said.

"No. It's not what I want, but a giant bottle of chilled orange juice isn't going to walk out of that forest."

"Not likely." He picked her up and brought her to the edge of the pool. She began scooping and slurping with her frail hands. After a few minutes, she rested her head on her arm. "Oh God, that was sooo good."

The way she'd said it evoked a highly sexual image of him on top of her naked body, pounding himself between her thighs, cumming inside her while she—

"Why are you looking at me like that?" Her voice was barely above a whisper, but there was an edge of panic in it.

"I wasn't looking at you." He moved to take her from the water's edge, but she held up her hand.

"Please don't touch me," she said.

"Why not?"

"You looked at me like… It was just strange; that's all."

"You're delusional."

She coughed. "Maybe I am. And maybe I should take my chances alone."

He shook his head. "I may be a coldhearted bastard, but I'm not a prick who's about to leave a sick woman in the middle of the forest." *Why the hell am I saying that? I am that sort of prick. I should leave her here. Send someone back for her later.*

But that wasn't what he wanted. He wanted to…

Keep her. You want to keep her. Don't fight it. Roen blinked and held in a sickness crawling up his throat. Those words had *not* come from him. Yet they had.

Roen cleared his throat, denying that what just happened was real. Because it wasn't. It had to be the damned stress getting to him. "By the way, in case you're wondering, this island is completely off the grid, out in the middle of the Pacific. You don't have a chance of leaving it without me."

"And if I refuse to go anywhere with you?" she muttered with eyes closed.

The sun had already begun to set and the temperature was dropping fast. These were not the tropics, and he guessed it would only get colder. They'd probably be warmer if they stuck near the ocean. "Then I'll take you with me anyway. Because while I'm a coldhearted bastard, I'm also a prick who listens to no one."

She chuckled underneath her breath. "You're a funny man, Roen."

"No. I'm not." He lifted her from the muck and sat her against a thick tree trunk again. He tried not to think about how good she felt in his arms and how touching her sent a quick rush of blood into his cock. Not enough to give him a raging erection, but certainly enough to let him know the damned thing was awake.

"I'm sorry I just said all that," she grumbled. "I think I'm in shock."

"Here," he said, handing her the apple he'd found in that small sack she'd carried with her, "you need to eat this."

She pushed it away. "I'm not hungry. I'm thirsty."

"Yes. You said that already. Eat the *foking* damned apple."

"Why do you sometimes have a Scottish accent when you swear?"

Roen inhaled an impatient breath and stood. He hated it when people asked him personal questions. His accent wasn't any of their damned business and why should they care? "I don't know what you're talking about." He went back to trying his phone.

Liv chuckled quietly underneath her breath. "Okay, *foking toof* guy."

Roen shot her a quick look of disapproval, but let it slide. He had more important things to worry about.

"At least tell me why you're helping me?" she asked in her faint voice. "I can tell it's not your style."

He frowned down at her. She knew nothing about his style. "I'm not a fan of men who hurt women. And I'm a lesser fan of watching people die."

Her large brown eyes opened and pinned him with her inquisitive gaze. "So you're a sentimental do-gooder."

Truth was, he'd hated seeing his mother always on the verge of a mental breakdown because his father didn't care enough to do right by her. It was what eventually broke her. So if there was one thing in this world that got under his skin, it was men like that. "I simply do not see the point in taking advantage of the weak."

"No, where's the fun in that?" she said sarcastically.

He smiled, masking the serious undertones of the conversational path they'd veered down. "Exactly. So who's Dana?" he asked, changing the subject.

"My sister. How'd you know her name? Was it in the papers?"

"You were mumbling something about her and a party. You also mentioned Krista likes to keep company with penguins."

Liv made a little laugh. "I must've been talking about my parents' fortieth wedding anniversary. It's in a few months. Dana—my younger sister—and I have been helping with the planning."

"And Krista?" he asked.

"My older sister. She lives in Portland and works at the zoo. How about your family? Any brothers or sisters?"

"No. No family," he replied curtly. "None who are alive, anyway." Why were they back to speaking about his personal life?

Because I brought it up. Which, in itself, was odd. He rarely felt any curiosity regarding the personal lives of others. He simply never saw the point when he had no interest in getting close to anyone.

"I'm sorry to hear that," Liv said with heartfelt sympathy. "It must be hard."

"Trust me, my life is nothing to pity."

"No—I didn't mean it like that," she said, flicking a fallen pine needle from her lap. "It's just I can see you were probably good at it."

"At what?" he asked.

She flashed a little smile up at him. "Taking care of them, protecting them. I bet you miss it."

He'd never thought about it and had no desire to start now. "I thought you said that caring about others wasn't my style."

She shrugged a little. "That was a test to see what you'd say."

Normally, he'd tell people like her—the prying, prodding kind—to go fuck themselves, but he found her oddly enticing, which is why he simply stared at her, mentally scratching his head.

"Sorry," she said. "I crossed the line, didn't I?"

"Yes." He smiled.

She shook her head at herself. "I'm sorry. I've spent so much of my life thinking about how people's connections mold their lives and who they are, I'm hardwired now to try to figure everyone out."

He folded his arms over his chest. "And what have you figured out?"

She placed her hands in her lap and stared at them for a moment with tired eyes. He suddenly wondered what she might be like when she wasn't feeling so weak. *I bet she's a handful.* Something he liked the idea of, to be frank.

"I think," she said, "that you are possibly the most misjudged man I've ever met."

He laughed. "Really now? Why's that?"

"Because your face is the least beautiful thing about you."

What sort of bloody line was that? "What game are you playing, Miss Stratton? You don't even know me."

She huffed and then looked up at him with such intense emotion it halted his breathing for a moment. "No games, Mr. Doran. I happen to be exceptionally good at reading people. And I might not make it to morning, so I thought I should tell you the truth since you asked."

Roen's heart pounded and his body filled with a wave of indescribable, overwhelming emotion, somewhere between anger and excitement. Who the hell was this woman? And why did she have such an effect on him? It was like she'd just reached right inside and started stirring him around.

Because she's yours. Claim her before someone else does.

Roen froze, unsure if he'd really heard the voice or if it was his own thoughts bubbling up to the surface.

"What did you just say?" Liv asked, clearly alarmed.

"I didn't say anything."

"Yes. You did," she argued. "You gave me that weird look again and said that I belong to you."

No, he hadn't. "I have no idea what you're talking about. I just met you, and I'm not the sort of man who wants to own anyone. I rent at best, but never own."

Yours. All yours, said the voice.

"Stop," he said.

She blinked. "Stop what?"

Jesus, I'm losing my mind. "I'm not interested in you."

Her jaw dropped. "You think I was just flirting with you?"

No. But he had to say something. Because something was...wrong. Very wrong. "If I want a woman, I tell her."

She scowled. "I wasn't flirting with you, you idiot—are you all right?"

Suddenly, they both saw a flare sail through the early evening sky.

"It came from the shore," he said. Likely close to the spot where the helicopter had gone down. His crew probably assumed he was somewhere on the island. If they could even see the island. He still didn't understand how this damned place wasn't visible until they were right on top of it.

He blew out a breath. Lucky for him, he was in great shape due to his daily, two-hour workout regimen of weights and cardio. Because now he would have to carry Liv back to the beach and hope his people were still there in an hour.

His phone suddenly vibrated in his pocket. He quickly dug it out, seeing it was his ship's captain. *About time.*

"Hello?" Roan said, but no one replied. "Hello?" Roen repeated several more times.

"What the fuck do you think you're doing with that?" said a strange male voice from behind him.

Roen swiveled on his heel, finding the man he'd hit over the head earlier, accompanied by nine others. Unfortunately for him, they were all taller than his six-six height and probably double in muscle mass, which said a lot. Roen was no scrawny runt. Not that size could trump the razor-sharp machetes each man carried.

"I'm guessing you're not here to offer us welcome mai tais," Roen said, while quickly assessing each man, trying to determine what he was dealing with.

You're in deep shit. That's what you're dealing with. The colossal men with long hair—some with dreads—wore nothing but black cloths around their waists. Some had elaborate black tribal tattoos—fish scales, sea monsters, tridents—over a good

portion of their excessively ripped bodies. And from
the ferocious look in their light eyes, they were not
the sort to shy away from a little bloodshed.

"Sorry," said one of the men toward the back,
"you missed cocktail hour."

Roen cracked his neck. "So then why the fuck
are you here?"

The man who'd attacked Liv scratched his
bearded chin. "I asked you a question, pretty boy.
Who said you were allowed to make calls from our
island?"

The men exchanged glances, grinning at each
other.

Pretty boy? Last time he'd checked, he was
anything but that. *A good-looking asshole maybe.*
Either way, who were these guys? Perhaps
mercenaries paid to protect this island from
intruders.

In those outfits? Not likely.

"Who's asking?" Roen said, hoping to get some
sort of clue as to what they wanted and intended to
do—kill them, take them as prisoners, or send them
on their way.

"My name is Shane," he answered with an evil
gloating grin. "And you?"

"I'm the guy who has no issues with you," Roen
said, "but could change his mind."

Shane glanced down at Liv. "Go ahead. Change
your mind. Because someone attacked me, and
you're now in possession of our property."

So Liv hadn't been exaggerating. They truly believed she belonged to them. *We're definitely not being sent on our way.*

Suddenly, that strange voice inside Roen's head began clawing at him, demanding blood. *She is yours. Not theirs. Don't let them take her.*

This time, Roen didn't fight it. In fact, he felt empowered by it. "The woman is with me," he growled. "So take me to whoever's in charge, because I'm not about to let anyone touch what's mine."

Shane chuckled. "You think you're in a position to make demands?"

All right. Shane wasn't the true leader; otherwise he would have said so. His ego would have demanded it. Roen also knew that men like these—thugs—only respected one thing in life: power.

"Yes, and I've got a ship full of armed men," Roen bluffed, "who are now on your beach and would agree with my right to demand."

"You have men? On our beach?" Shane asked, seeming amused.

"Not for long," one of the long-haired assholes said before they all burst into laughter.

"Anyone want to take an evening dip?" another said, roaring hysterically.

Christ. Roen wasn't sure what they meant, but these bastards were mad. Completely mad. But he couldn't let that rattle him.

"If you clowns are finished, I'd like to speak to the poor bastard who gets the honor of calling himself your leader," Roen said.

The men fell silent.

"I think your words are naively tough for a man in your position." Shane stepped forward as if he was about to take a swing with his machete, when one of the others pulled him back.

"No. Let's give the landlover what he wants. Let him meet with L'isle," he said.

Shane grinned. "This piece of shit isn't worthy of L'isle's time. But"—he looked at Roen—"leave the woman, and you can go back where you came from. With your *men*." He grinned smugly, clearly knowing something Roen did not.

The group of thugs chuckled again.

Roen shook his head. He didn't want to fight ten guys who happened to be larger than him, but that was Roen's Achilles' heel: He'd rather die than let anyone step on him. Living one year in group homes after his mother died, where he'd had his ass kicked every day by the other boys, taught him one thing: Backing down only invited more sadistic bastards to knock you around, kick you in the balls until you cough up blood, and hit your nose so many times that even four surgeries couldn't completely put it back straight.

Roen clenched his fists. "As I said, she's mine. So you have two choices: touch her and die. Or touch me and die."

The men burst out laughing, but Roen didn't give a damn. No, he wouldn't win this fight, but he'd take at least one of these skirt-wearing fuckers with him. If anything, he might be able to provide a distraction to allow Liv to escape. The blunt, ugly truth was that no one would give a shit if he died. But Liv had an entire family waiting to see her again. Simply put, her life mattered more than his.

Roen almost choked on his uncharacteristically selfless thoughts. *Hell, Roen, something is very, seriously the matter with you.*

Shane crossed his arms, snickering. "All right, tough guy. You're obviously lost and arrived on our island by mistake. But you're in luck; we happen to be feeling generous today. Prove she's yours, and you may take her."

"What proof do you want?" Roen scoffed.

"Call her. Make her crawl to you and kiss your foot."

Roen wanted to kill the guy for merely suggesting it. "I think you can go and f—"

"No. It's okay," Liv interrupted. Her fearful eyes blinked at him, then quickly swept over the savage faces standing around them. "I'm yours. I don't mind proving it." Her voice was low and scratchy. Roen knew it wasn't meant to be sexy, but it still came out that way.

You're a sick bastard, he thought to himself.

Liv slowly moved to her hands and knees, her gaze fixed on Roen's eyes. He knew in her weakened state, doing this took everything she had. But in the short time he'd known her, he'd already figured out she was a fighter. *And clever and sexy.*

Liv began crawling toward him, and with every inch, Roen's blood simmered hotter and hotter. Partially because it pissed him off that these men wanted to humiliate her, but also because seeing the top of her full breasts pushing against the confines of her tattered T-shirt, her pert ass pushed slightly into the air, made him see images of her crawling toward him on a bed. Naked, sweaty, and ready.

Roen pushed back the lustful thoughts. This wasn't the time or place. However, as Liv bent her head down and kissed the top of his foot, the softness of her plump lips jarred him. *Jesus, fucking hell, woman.* If kissing his foot felt this good, he could only imagine how good her mouth would feel on the tip of his—

You're a dirty bastard, Roen. A coldhearted bastard.

Roen was only vaguely aware of the men around him, who watched with a predatory fascination as Liv leaned back and raised herself onto her knees, smiling up at him. "Was that good?"

You have no idea. It was quite possibly the most erotic thing a woman had ever done to him. And he didn't even have a foot fetish.

"Not good enough. Have the little whore suck your cock," said Shane.

Roen's and Liv's heads swiveled in shock.

"You're a disgusting pig!" Liv barked.

Shane flashed a sadistic smile. "As I thought. You're not his."

Liv hissed, "Just because I'm not in favor of public blowjobs doesn't mean—"

"Liv," Roen cut her off, "we both know that's not true."

Liv's nostril's flared with outrage.

Roen leaned down to Liv, who remained kneeling at his feet. "Liv," he whispered, placing his hand on her cheek, pretending like he was going to talk her into their contemptible request. "You were right. You are good at reading people."

Liv's confused expression indicated she was probably wondering why he'd just said that.

Roen quickly kissed her lips. "Now, I want you to do me a favor and run like hell."

Roen turned and lunged for Shane, knocking him to the ground. The men descended upon him and threw him to the ground. Roen swung, making contact with one, but it did no good.

"No!" Liv screamed. "Don't touch him!"

Why the hell hadn't she run? Roen only caught a glimpse of her tortured expression, her hand reaching for him, before one of the men kicked his head.

CHAPTER FIVE

"Stop! You're going to kill him." Liv watched in horror while ten extremely large men kicked Roen's ribs, back, and head with their bare feet.

Weaker than hell, she managed to stand and throw herself at one of the men, but he flung her back, sending her crashing into a tree trunk.

Liv gulped for air, the skin on her back burning, while they laughed and carried out the vicious assault, thoroughly enjoying the sound of cracking bones and the sight of Roen bleeding. She didn't know the man, but no one deserved to die like this. No one.

As soon as her breath returned, she screamed, "Roen! Roen—oh God. Roen!"

One of the men, a blond with a long braid down his back and a giant sea serpent tattooed on his chest, looked at her. "His name is Roen?"

"Yes." She nodded frantically. "Roen Doran."

His green eyes lit up. "Fuck." He turned to the other men and started pushing a few back. "Stop, you fucking idiots! He's Roen Doran."

The nine other men froze, shock in their eyes. Shane stared down at the bloody heap on the ground, stepping away as if Roen carried Ebola. "This guy? It's not possible."

How they knew Roen or why it resulted in their sudden fear of him didn't matter. They'd stopped kicking.

"Yes! He's Roen Doran. I swear it," Liv said.

Shane shot her a worried look. "How did he arrive here?"

"His ship. It's a few miles offshore."

The group of men exchanged uneasy glances.

"We have to get him to the great hall before L'isle sees this," one of the men said.

Shane nodded. "You do that. But don't give him too much water. He's not one of us. Not yet, anyway."

Oh shit. They planned to make Roen one of them? What the hell did that even mean?

"Put this one in a cage until the claiming tonight." Shane jerked his head toward Liv.

Liv held up her hands as the blond approached her. "Sonofabitch, you fucking touch me," she growled, "and I swear I'll kill you." Yeah, that was a pretty empty threat given she didn't possess a really, really big army or elephant tranquilizers.

The blond guy with the braid cocked his head and flashed a set of pristine white teeth. "I like feisty women with dirty mouths. Maybe I'll put my name in the hat for you." He plucked her off the ground by the arms and began dragging her by the wrist through the forest, while the others lifted Roen and disappeared in the opposite direction.

Where were they taking him? What were they going to do to him? She'd only just met Roen, but the way he'd stood up to these horrible cretins left her feeling...well, she didn't really know. Loyal, attached, indebted, turned on, shocked as hell? All of the above?

Roen was not the depthless, coldhearted playboy the media portrayed. He was altogether something different, almost another species of man entirely— the sort that exuded a fearless, raw, masculine energy that could just as easily scare the crap out of you as it could leave your body breathless with need.

No wonder women trip over themselves for a night with this guy. Just one look at those piercing green eyes, just one glimpse of that strong jaw and broad shoulders and you wanted to be anything, say anything, do anything to be his even if only for a few hours. Not that she wanted that. Because...they didn't know each other. And it would be insane to have carnal urges for a man she barely knew. During a life-or-death situation. When she hadn't showered in over ten days and suffered from dehydration.

But Holy Christ, that kiss. It was only a peck, but it left her wanting and needing so much more.

Then he'd thrown himself to the wolves in an attempt to set her free. No one had ever stood up for her like that—not that she needed a man to protect her, but still. She couldn't remember anyone ever really trying. Not even her ex, some loser named Dan she'd dated during her second and third year of college, lifted a finger when they'd been at a bar one night and some drunk jerk grabbed her ass on the way to the bathroom. She'd confronted the guy and told him to keep his hands to himself, to which he'd responded, "Wow. You're a real bitch. Someone needs to give you a good fuck." Furious as hell, she slapped the dipshit and then went back to the table and told Dan she wanted to leave. Later, Dan would mention he saw the entire thing from across the room and thought it was funny. *Funny? He saw the entire thing and did nothing?* Not that she wanted Dan getting into a barroom brawl, but not giving a crap wasn't the correct response either, which was why she dumped Dan that same night. Strong woman or not, she could only love a man who...

Acted like Roen just did?

Okay, she didn't love the man, but for whatever reason, she'd been unable to run when he told her to. All she'd thought about was how she had to stop those pigs from hurting him and how they were trying to take something away from her—a prized possession she had every right to keep. *Just like right now.* The idea of anyone laying their filthy fucking hands on that man sent her into an epic womanly rage.

"You can't take me away. I belong to Roen," Liv blurted out. She had no clue if that might persuade him not to separate them, but it was worth a shot.

The blond man chuckled. "Now, now. We both know that's a lie."

Barely able to support her own weight, Liv stumbled behind him over fallen branches, slippery pine needles, and mushy leaves, trying to keep pace with the gargantuan man. "But you heard him say it," she panted.

"Trust me; if you were really his—or any of ours—we'd know."

"How?" she asked.

He laughed. "You'll find out soon enough, darlin'."

She didn't like the sound of that. "You mean, I'll know after I'm claimed by one of you?"

"That's right."

"What's going to be done to me?" she panted, hoping it might help prepare her to fight.

He laughed. "Oh. Well, that depends on what you like. Most of us are game for anything, especially when it comes to a beautiful woman. Although, I did have a woman once ask me to wear a Little Bo Peep costume, so I had to draw the line. But the Zorro outfit was fun."

This conversation was not only surreal, it made no sense. He spoke as if *she* would be asking one of these men to sexually role-play. They were all completely out of their minds, but pointing out that fact was useless.

She was about to ask if Roen would be all right
and where they were taking him when she suddenly
felt a black curtain pull over her eyes, her body
slamming into the ground.

"Woman, wake the fuck up." A sharp slap across
her cheek jolted her into consciousness.

She sucked in a breath and saw the blond man
kneeling over her.

"What happened?" she muttered. The canopy of
deep green trees above were no longer visible—too
dark now—nevertheless, the world seemed to move
in one giant nauseating wave.

"You passed out. Didn't Shane give you the
sacred water?"

She rubbed her eyes. "You mean that weird stuff
laced with speed?"

"Yes. Though, there are no drugs in it."

"He gave me a whole pouch of it." She left out
the fact that she'd taken another small bottle of it
from Shane's home. "What's in it?"

The man frowned. "And you still do not feel
well?"

Why wouldn't he answer her damned question?
"No. I'm dehydrated. I need water. Real water."

He scratched his jaw. "I think you need to see
our doctor." He scooped her up into his arms.

"Is he a real doctor, or do you just call him that?"

He marched through the forest at a swift pace,
ducking beneath small branches, unaffected by the
waning light or carrying her.

Must be that water. That and like the other men
she'd seen, his height easily pushed seven feet. His

arms and legs bulged with taut tattoo-covered muscles. Also like the other men, he was unusually handsome despite the bushy beard and unkempt hair. No. She wasn't attracted to him, but it struck her as odd. All of the men seemed to be cut from the same fabric—large, built, better than average good-looking, and green eyes. There was something very, very different about this lot.

"Our doctor went to Harvard," the man said.

Harvard?

"Though these days," he continued, "he spends most of his time fishing—not much healing to do around here except when the women come. Then there's a hell of a lot of broken bones."

Oh shit. "Broken bones?"

"Never mind. You just watch your manners." He gave her a little squeeze to remind her that he was in a position to inflict serious damage.

Regardless, she couldn't "never mind" that. She was scared out of her ever-loving head. *I need to find Roen and get the hell out of here.*

"Will Roen be there, too?" she asked.

"Why would he be?" he said.

"He's bleeding. You kicked his nose in and God knows what else." *Kidneys, broken spine...*

"We were just playing around. He'll be fine," the man said casually.

They sure as hell were *not* playing around. They'd meant to kill him. "You're going to give him that water, aren't you?" It had healed her cuts, so she had to assume it would heal his, too.

The man glanced down at her disapprovingly. "You ask a lot of questions. Maybe I won't put my name in the hat."

Woe is me. A huge loss, surely. "If asking questions is a turnoff, then what's your name? Who are you people? Why are you such assholes who feel the need to beat up on women?"

"We don't beat up women." He seemed genuinely offended.

Like hell they didn't. In fact, she had a lovely sore spot on the back of her neck where Shane had grabbed her while he'd been shoving her head under water. "You just told me you have a doctor for their broken bones."

"That's for our men. Bones need to be set properly before they drink the—You know what? Never mind. Stop talking."

Okay. Liv wondered why the men would be breaking each other's bones for the women that came there. It had to be part of that "claiming" she'd heard Shane speaking of earlier. But what sort of women would want to come to this place? *Maybe they're all insane women with nowhere else to go. Or maybe they don't come here voluntarily.* Now that she could believe.

"If I weren't so dehydrated, I'd spit on you," she said.

The man shook his head and kept walking through the dark forest. Meanwhile, she tried her best to keep her head on straight. Not easy to do given how badly her body ached and her stomach hurt. She truly needed to be in a hospital. Her heart fluttered away, working overtime to pump the overly thick blood and carry oxygen to her vital organs. And the temperature of the air had dipped about twenty degrees in the last thirty minutes. She'd grown up in the small town of Wrangell, Alaska, where peak temperatures ranged in the low sixties, but despite being accustomed to the cold, she couldn't stop shivering.

Just hang on. If there was a real doctor on the island, he might help her. Then again, maybe not. He was a doctor. On *this* island.

Ten minutes later, they arrived at a cottage in a small clearing. And while the cottage didn't have French windows like Shane's home, this one had lights all around the exterior and a satellite dish on the overhang above the front door.

Harvard doctor and a TV dish. Who the hell are these people? They weren't as primitive as they appeared; however, given her background in sociology, which included a master's in cultural anthropology, she'd already noted how their pecking order and rules resembled more of a tribal society with one primary leader: this L'isle man they'd mentioned. But why would men who seemed so savage and isolated have modern equipment and speak perfect English?

"What?" The front door flew open, and the man who answered was just as large as the rest, about seven feet tall, but with long, wild curly red hair and pale green eyes. He wore a red—not black—cloth around his waist and had no body art.

"What the hell do you want, Jason?" said the redhead.

So blond-guy who'd been carrying her was Jason.

"Hey, fucker." Jason set Liv down on her feet and gripped her arm, pushing her forward. "This landlover drifted ashore during Shane's watch. She's a companion of Roen Doran—he's here on the island."

The redheaded man's expression soured. "Another Doran? Is here?"

With the driest tone known to man, Jason said, "No, Holden. I just said that name because I'm a joker. Next, I'm going to juggle. Your spleen."

The man standing in the doorway, Holden, scratched his short, scruffy, red beard and ignored the threat. "I don't think we've ever seen this happen."

Liv was careful not to move or breathe or do anything to stop their conversation. She wanted any information about these guys she could get.

"What do you think it means?" Holden added.

Jason shook his head. "Having two chiefs on the island at the same time can only mean one thing."

Chief. They thought Roen was one of their leaders. *What the hell?*

Holden bobbed his thick head of wild red hair. "It means war."

Jason grinned. "About fucking time."

"Why would you say that?" Holden replied disgustedly.

"Some of us have been training for hundreds of years," said Jason. "What's the use of owning party clothes if you're not going to the dance?"

Hundreds of years, Liv thought. *That doesn't make sense.*

Holden folded his thick, ripped arms, and Liv noticed him pushing out his chest. "If the scriptures are correct, we all die. Not just the men and our maids, but the landlovers, too." Holden took a step outside his cottage, just inches from Jason. "So think long and hard, Jason, about what you're rooting for."

"I root for anything that will end my suffering," Jason said.

"She can be brought back," Holden replied. "You simply have to be patient. And everyone must do their part to avoid a conflict when the time comes."

Jason shook his head. "You're wrong. She's gone. And there's no point hoping for anything else. No one will be free until we're all dead and this goddamned place sinks to the bottom of the ocean."

"Only a selfish asshole would wish his people dead, Jason."

Jason pushed Holden, and Holden stumbled back a few feet into his doorway.

Shit. Liv felt her knees wobbling and her vision blinking out. "Hey," she coughed out. "If you let me die, Roen won't be happy." It was a gamble that these men would even care, but they did seem to think Roen was someone important. A chief.

Both men stopped and looked at her.

Ohmygod. It worked.

"Please, I just need help," she said. *And I need to find Roen. Please let him be all right.* Of course, she also knew she needed to be careful around Roen, too. The way he'd looked at her before those men had shown up set off alarm bells all over her body. At the same time, there was something about his possessive, hungry gaze that…that…*did* something to her. It was the strangest damned thing.

"Get the hell back on your side of the island," Holden said to Jason, and then he grabbed Liv's wrist and pulled her inside the cottage before slamming the door in Jason's face.

Holden's bare, chiseled chest rose and fell rapidly while he spewed profanities at the shut door.

"Do you have any water? Real water?" she asked.

Holden shook his head from side to side to compose himself. "Yes, of course. Right this way." He led her into a small, but modern kitchen— granite counters, stainless steel appliances, glass cooktop.

This looks like my mom's kitchen. Right down to the gray frosted-glass tile she'd had put in a few months ago as an early anniversary gift from her father. The puzzle of who these men really were kept getting bigger and messier.

He gestured for her to sit at a round breakfast table in the corner and then brought over a glass pitcher from the counter. He poured her a mug and handed it to her. Of course, she emptied the thing in one giant swallow.

"Can I have more?" She held out the empty mug with her shaking hand.

He refilled it, and she greedily drank it down, her eyes rolling in the back of her head. Water had never tasted so sweet.

"Thank you." She set the empty mug down and then licked her lips.

Holden simply stared at her with curiosity. "So what brings you to our island?"

"I was shipwrecked."

"And you drifted *here*?" There was a large dose of disbelief served with the question, which made her not want to answer. These people were quick to assign significance to everything. Including her.

"Can I have more water?" she said, to change the subject. "I haven't had much to drink in five days."

"Did anyone give you the other water we have on this island?"

She nodded. "Yes. What was in it?"

"You still feel ill?"

She nodded again.

He frowned and scratched his jaw. "No one knows what's in it, but..." He kneeled in front of her and pulled down her lower lid. "Yes, I can see you're still mildly dehydrated. And you're *sure* you drank *our* water?"

"Yes. It healed my skin and made me feel good for a few minutes, but it wore off. And what do you mean you don't know what's in it?"

He shook his head. "There are many mysteries on this island, one being the fact that the water doesn't seem to affect you like it does everyone else. May I try something?"

"If you give me more real water, yes."

"I'll give you juice in a few minutes. We don't want to overwhelm your system."

"What do you want to try?" she asked.

"This." He leaned forward and kissed her hard, cupping his hands on the sides of her head to keep her from jerking away. His soft lips moved over her mouth.

"Gek-oh-mi!" *Let go of me!* she mumbled into his mouth and used what little strength she had to push him away.

He pulled back and stared at her with his large, light green eyes. "How was that?"

"Why did you kiss me?" Her eyes started scanning the kitchen for knives or some other weapon.

"I wanted to see what happened," he replied.

"I'm terrified. That's what happened," she said bitterly.

He stood and then crossed his arms, staring down at her inquisitively. "You seem to be immune to us, too."

"What sort of reaction were you expecting?"

"Let's get you to my exam room."

Hell no! She jerked back in her chair, readying to run for the door. Not that she'd get far, but they were all completely out of their minds.

He gave her a look. "I won't harm you. I promise. My job is helping people, not killing them. That's why I'm a doctor."

"Did you really go to Harvard?"

"I know I don't fit the image." He swept his hand over his large, muscular, nearly nude body. "But nothing on this island is what it seems."

Liv remained glued to the chair, debating how far she'd get if she chucked her mug at him.

"Listen." Holden dropped his arms to his sides. "You don't have many options. You're on an island. You're sick. And, frankly—" His eyes stuck to her shirt. "Is that your blood?"

Liv slowly shook her head. "Shane killed a shark."

Holden smiled. "That explains the smell."

Liv didn't smile back.

"Okay. I'll make you a deal," he said, "let me do my job and help you. If you still want to run after I do, feel free. But we'd better hurry before Shane's men come back for you."

Maybe he was right. She needed to get stronger before she'd be in a position to fight or flee or find Roen. Still, she didn't want to go anywhere with this man.

As if he'd read her mind, he said, "I promise, no more kissing." He jerked his head, gesturing for her to follow. After a few moments, she hesitantly rose from the chair and walked down a narrow hallway into a small room with a gurney and modern medical equipment—heart monitor, oxygen tank, etc.

"Who are you people?" she asked.

"You'll get your answers in good time—by the way, what should I call you?"

"Liv."

He helped her onto the exam table and wrapped a band around her arm to take her blood pressure. "How did you meet Roen?"

She didn't want to say anything that might undermine her story of belonging to him. "That doesn't matter. But I'm his."

Holden gave her a look. "Word of advice, Liv. Lying is a serious offense on this island. Especially if you're a landlover. Stick to the truth, and you'll have a better chance of staying alive."

His words hit her panic button. Yes, she knew she wasn't safe, but hearing him say they might kill her cemented that assumption right into the ground. She needed to pump this man for as much information as she could get.

He finished checking her pressure and then removed the band. "I'm going to put you on an IV and give you some more liquids. I think you'll live, though."

"How do you know I'm lying about Roen?"

"Because when a woman has been claimed, there are clear physical signs—none of which you have."

This was ludicrous. "Do you brand them, rip out their tongues, what?"

"No. I'll be right back with your juice. You just focus on resting."

Rest. Yeah, right. She was stuck on an island in the most surreal situation she could ever imagine. *No, actually. You couldn't imagine. Not in a million years.*

"Whoever you people are," she said bitterly, "whatever you're planning to do to me isn't right. And I think you know it."

Holden stopped in the doorway, his broad bare back to her. "Sorry," he said with regret, "but you belong to the island now. Right and wrong don't exist, only our laws do." He then disappeared.

Okay. Liv had to start her plan of attack immediately. They were never going to let her go. But the other guy, Jason, had said he'd been with women. As in multiples. So if women came to this island and never left, where were they?

Dead. It's the only thing that makes sense. He and Holden had spoken about some woman Jason had lost. And then that guy Shane had said there was only one way off the island for women. Her first thought had been "in a body bag," so this confirmed it. They probably sacrificed the women or mutilated them or... *Fuck. Something not-awesome.*

Liv needed to get the hell out of there, which meant finding Roen because his ship was her only way home. However, that wasn't the only reason. As strange as it sounded, she'd do just about anything to see him again and make sure he was all right. Even if it meant risking her own life.

That thought steamrolled right over her. Liv had always been generous with her heart, including when it came to helping strangers. But this thing with Roen felt so vastly different. It felt intense and magnetic and, well, deeply carnal. It was like Roen had reached inside her and touched a part of her soul she hadn't even known existed.

Liv covered her face with both hands, groaning inwardly. *Get a hold of yourself, Liv. It's just the situation. Nothing more.*

Regardless, she still owed it to Roen to help him, just like he'd helped her. As soon as she was able to stand straight, she would run for it and find him.

Hell or high water, we are getting off this damned island.

$\approx$

Roen awoke in a soft warm bed and stretched his body. It took a moment to register he was no longer in the mud being attacked by a group of ruthless barbarians.

He reached for the back of his head and warily touched the spot where he remembered receiving the first blow. There was no bump. Not even a bruise.

How's that possible? The only explanation was that they'd given him that damned water. What the hell was in it? Whatever the case, people would kill, maim, and fight like hell to get their hands on something like that.

Roen slowly sat up, feeling a bit light-headed, and assessed the rest of his body. Naked body. *Where the hell are my clothes?*

Then he remembered something else that was missing: *Liv.* His heart began thumping wildly inside his chest.

Sonsofbitches. The thought of those vile assholes touching her sent a wild, possessive rage charging through him. No. He didn't really know the woman, but she was his. And only his.

Roen shook his head. *Mine? What the hell's gotten into me*? He was acting like a wild lion who'd had his kill stolen by a pack of hyenas. Liv was not his. *This place is fucking with my bloody head.* Still, savage animal-like feelings or not, he couldn't let them do whatever they liked to her.

Wincing from a few tender spots along his rib cage, he slowly stood from the narrow bed and looked around the empty room. There wasn't much except the drawn white curtains, paneled walls and the bed. He grabbed the bed sheet and wrapped it around his waist, placing his ear to the door before going out.

Nothing.

Slowly, he cracked open the door and tiptoed down the short hallway that led to a small living room. Aside from a wall of shelving filled with dusty books, there were two brown leather reading chairs, one occupied by a sleeping, scrawny old man wearing nothing but a piece of suede around his waist. His long gray hair cascaded down his bare shoulders and his scraggly silver beard reached his belly.

"Good. You're awake," the old man said in a scratchy, worn voice, leaving his eyes closed. "There are bands on the bottom shelf. You may pick whichever color you like."

Roen's eyes followed the man's pointing finger to several stacks of folded red and black cloths. "Where is the woman I was with?" Roen snatched up a red cloth. He'd be damned if he went after Liv in a bed sheet.

"She's with our healer." The old man opened his dark green eyes and gestured toward the empty chair.

A healer? "What did you do to her?"

The old man bobbed his head. "I understand why you might think that of us, but we have our laws when it comes to women. Laws you'll learn about soon enough."

"Meaning I should simply trust that she's not harmed—"

"She is not," the old man interrupted.

"Or won't be harmed?"

"I didn't say that. I said we have laws. One of which is that women must give themselves willingly on this island, so you needn't worry about that."

When it came to this island, everything worried him. "I want to see her."

"As I said, she's resting, being treated for dehydration, and won't be ready until tonight."

Ready for fucking what?

"Come sit." He gestured again toward the chair. "There is much to discuss."

Roen didn't have the patience for this conversation. God only knew what these savages were doing to Liv.

He moved to the door and pulled it open. Outside stood six very large men with long black hair and scale tattoos from their torsos down to their bare feet. They wore black cloths around their waists and held very sharp machetes.

Great. More of them. Roen rubbed his forehead. Obviously, he wasn't going anywhere, and picking a fight with these men would earn him another beating. He'd be no use to Liv that way.

Roen slowly turned and walked over to the empty chair, the old man's watchful gaze studying his every move.

"If I sit," Roen said, "and have this conversation, will you let me leave and see the woman?"

The man smiled, revealing a set of very white teeth. "You are not our prisoner."

"So I can go anytime I like?" Roen didn't believe that for one second.

"The island decides who stays and who goes. However, I have a feeling, my dear boy, that the island isn't done with you yet."

All right. So everyone in this place is insane. He wasn't surprised. After all, his father was the one who'd led him here. It made sense, frankly.

"And what do you believe the island wants to do with me?" Roen asked, expecting nothing less than a crazy answer to the crazy question.

"The same as everyone else who finds their way here: she wants you to take your place."

Crazy fuck. Roen clapped his hands together and stood. "It's been a pleasure conversing with you, but I—"

"What do you know about your father's relationship to this island?"

Roen's best guess was that his father had gotten mixed up with these people just as he had with fifty other "Mother Earth" cults, environmental terrorists (who paraded around as green advocates), and other subversives he thought might be useful in carrying out his deranged plots to save the planet.

"He told you that the island needs to be protected," said the old man.

"My father was insane," Roen pointed out.

"Was he?"

"Without a doubt." His father told anyone who'd listened that the ocean was dying and doomsday was coming. Because of this, he believed he had the right to kill, sabotage, and intimidate anyone he saw as the enemy—corporations who polluted the ocean, unscrupulous fishermen, even natural gas frackers who were responsible for releasing large quantities of methane—a compound that heavily contributes to global warming. He was arrested but never convicted of any crimes. Nevertheless, Roen knew, just like his mother and brother knew, that his father bombed factories, sank ships, and hired hackers to attack companies. People died because of him. Innocent people. And when some of those companies and families of those who died started coming after them—death threats, harassment, and having their home torched—Roen's mother did everything she could to keep him and his little brother safe. They ran. Several times. But eventually, his father would find them. Eventually, his father's enemies would, too. It was the stress and heartbreak that killed his mother. Of that he was sure.

"My father was a psychopath and a terrorist," said Roen.

The old man looked at him. "Your father did what the island told him to do."

Roen bobbed his head, unable to relate to the man's deep delusion.

"You do not believe me."

"Look—what's your name?" Roen asked.

"You may call me Naylor."

"All right, Naylor. Get to the point, because—"

The man held up his hand and leaned forward. "Silence, Roen. I see your father was right about you. You're too full of yourself. You're too used to getting things your way. But on this island, you're not king. You haven't earned your place yet."

Roen lost his patience, but did everything in his power not to show it. This was a game of chess where these strange men held most of the pieces and his only weapon was timing—waiting for the right moment to get the hell out of there. "What do you want?"

"First, I'd like you to sit. Then I'd like you to listen."

"And after that?" Roen asked.

"Then you choose."

CHAPTER SIX

Roen sat for over an hour while Naylor spoke of absolutely nothing. And when he said nothing, he meant *nothing*. Random garble about how certain plants obtain moisture by channeling the frost that forms on their leaves. That sports were theatrical events meant to fill a primal void created by the lack of bloodshed men craved. How *Aphidius ervi*, the parasitic wasp, had such a keen sense of smell that it could tell if a potential aphid host carried a certain bacteria that could harm its eggs.

"All very fascinating, Naylor. But what does any of this have to do with me?" Roen asked.

"The point, Roen, is that Mother Nature is not static. She is driven by the soul and life energy of this planet, and she will fight to survive just like any creature. She will kill to defend herself. She will adapt when necessary."

"And?"

"And you are one of her adaptations, Roen. As are all of the men on this island. We were created for one specific purpose: to serve her, to protect her most precious possession."

Roen gave him a slow nod. "I'm guessing you're about to tell me what that is."

"The island, Roen."

Every time he thought this place couldn't get more demented, it did.

"I see you still do not believe me." Naylor's voice crackled, and he hacked up a ball of phlegm, which he swallowed. "However, even you know the ocean is the source of all life. Without it, Earth would simply be a lifeless rock. But it is the ocean that brings us rain, that carries nutrients from one end to another, that breathes life into our world. It flows like a vast circulatory system similar to that of the human body. Even our very own veins carry the same solution of salt."

Roen was quickly losing his patience with this pointless, abstract, nature lecture that reminded him of his father. All he could think about was Liv and not just because he felt concerned for her safety. That look on her face, when those men had attacked, wouldn't stop gnawing at him.

"All right," Roen said. "So the ocean is a big pool of earth blood. What do you want? Money to save the planet? Because if that's what this is about, I can give you enough to hire an army of lawyers to stop whatever companies you're after or to build a wildlife refuge or whatever the hell you crazy bastards like. But it is truly time for me to—"

"You're missing the point, Roen. To keep breathing, to keep her blood flowing, she needs a heart. Just like you. She cannot survive without it."

Roen stared blankly, knowing the punchline to this sci-fi fantasy was right around the corner.

"This island is her heart," Naylor said. "And she has chosen our people to protect it."

All right. I didn't see that coming. These people were some sort of naturalist religious cult.

Naylor closed his eyes, tilted back his head, and inhaled deeply, seemingly in his own world. "If you quiet your mind, you can feel her pulse, her energy and life force beating all around us—inside us. Landlovers have not evolved to perceive this sort of energy, but we have."

"So you're saying you're not human."

"I'm saying that *we* are not."

We. He said "we." The man believes I'm one of them.

"Of course," Naylor continued, "we are related to humans. The first of both our kind crawled from the ocean's salty womb onto the shores of this very island. Eventually, they lost their tails as well as the ability to breathe underwater—similar to reptiles who were once fish. Some eventually left the island. Our ancestors, however, stayed behind, evolving separately from landlovers for a million years. Not so different from the creatures of the Galapagos, only our island is a part of us. Our island is alive and speaks her will."

"The island speaks to you."

Naylor nodded. "Have you not heard her voice? That little whisper in the back of your mind that you cannot explain?"

Yes, he had. But...

Naylor held up his hand. "It is a shock for everyone when they find their way here, but I trust you'll adjust with time and find your place. You are a Doran."

"Meaning?"

"A Doran has led us since our ancestors slithered onto shore. The island always chooses a Doran. Always."

"You think I'm here to lead you?"

Naylor nodded. "Like everyone who is brought here, the island sees a purpose for you. Of course, we haven't had two Dorans on the island at once for a few thousand years—she has always brought our new leader after one dies. So I suppose you'll have to fight for the position."

His words were like the cherry on top of the crazy-bastard cake. As for whichever Doran was on this island—there were many Dorans in the world— he could have it. "If I don't fight? If I choose to leave?"

"You can't run from who you are."

"I'm Roen Doran. I own a ten-billion-dollar company that I built with my own two hands. I have a life, and it's not here."

"No. That Roen is a façade, a mask. The real man, the man you were born to be, is just beginning to work his way to the surface. You can run back to your old life, and you can pretend, but from the moment you stepped foot on the island and sipped our sacred water, the real you began to awaken."

Roen stood. "All right. I listened. Now I'm choosing: to leave. And I'm taking the woman with me."

"She is not yours for the taking."

"Then whose is she?" Roen asked, tamping down the anger building inside.

"The island will decide tonight during the claiming ceremony. Anyone who wishes to place their claim on her may step up to fight."

"You're all a bunch of sick bastards."

"What's sick is your naivety and blindness." Naylor stood from his chair with a quick motion. It was then Roen noticed the man might look old and feeble on the outside, but his gestures and mental sharpness were not. "How do you think your company became so big, Roen? Have you ever asked yourself that?"

"Hard work."

"Perhaps, yes, but it's no coincidence that your ships always find themselves welcomed by the ocean's peaceful waters and have never been attacked. Not even in Somalia. The island looks after her own. She's looked after you."

"We have armed escorts through international waters. It discourages pirates. And I just had a ship go down a few weeks ago."

Naylor smiled. "Yes. In a freak storm. A storm that ultimately led you here. Because it was time for you to return home."

"This isn't my home."

"You were conceived here like the rest of us. And like everyone else, she called you back to serve. Do not deny you felt her flowing through your veins, pulling you home."

What he'd felt was a sense that something bad was about to happen. And it had. Now it was time for him to leave. With Liv. Even if that meant calling his ship and bringing men back to take her by force.

"I listened. I chose. I want my cell so I can call my people," Roen growled.

"Aren't you going to stay and place a claim on the lovely woman? I hear she has twenty suitors fighting for the pleasure of bedding her this evening."

Every cell in Roen's body filled with rage. The thought of anyone touching her made his blood sizzle.

"The island brought her here," Naylor added, "which means she's special and makes her quite the catch. It's never happened before. Not once."

That made no sense to Roen, but nothing here did. "If anyone lays a finger on her, I'll kill them."

"One man against us all? I think even you, Roen, recognize a battle you cannot win. And if you plan to leave and return with some of those men from your ship, think again. The island's defenses go far beyond a few hundred very cutthroat men. You'd need ten armies to overtake us, and by the time you return for Liv, she will have spent the night enjoying another man's cock between her legs and possibly have his seed in her belly." Naylor pointed his finger at Roen. "The moment for killing and fighting will be tonight."

So they're all a bunch of ocean-hugging rapist psychopaths who enjoy killing each other. Roen wanted to light a match to this entire hellhole of an island.

Roen rubbed his lightly stubbled jaw. "I have to thank you. Because before I found this place, I believed I was one fucked-up, heartless sonofabitch. But after meeting you gentlemen, I feel like a goddamned saint. Of course, you set the bar so low given how you're all serial rapists, but still. It's nice to feel like the good guy for once."

Naylor laughed. "I'm going to enjoy watching the island tame you, Roen. You're like a wild beast begging to be broken in. But you'll come around. The island always gets what she wants. As for the female, I assure you that Liv will be in the giving mood for the man who wins her. I bet she'll give nicely too once she's recuperated a bit. Maybe I'll take a run for her myself since I hear that she looks like she knows her way around a hard cock."

Roen swung and landed his fist on Naylor's jaw, knocking him to the ground.

Naylor grunted as his head hit the ground with a thump and Roen jumped on top to wrap his hands around Naylor's neck. "I'll fucking kill you!" The men from outside burst into the room.

"No!" Naylor held up his hand. "He's still a weak landlover. He's not hurting me."

He wasn't?

Roen squeezed with all his strength, but the man's neck felt like solid rock. "What are you?" he whispered.

Naylor grinned. "Same as you, Roen. We are the sons of the sea. We are mermen."

Roen jerked his head. *Mermen?* "You're fucking insane."

"We may have lost our tails, but that doesn't change who we are, Roen." He glanced at the men. "Remove Mr. Doran and show him to the shore."

"Why?" one of the men asked nervously.

"He says he wants to leave—" Naylor flashed a wicked grin "—so let the man leave. He can swim home."

The men grabbed Roen and yanked him to his feet.

"I'm not leaving without Liv," Roen grunted, trying to yank back his arms.

Naylor nodded, and the men dragged Roen outside through a short stretch of forest to the rocky shore. It was so dark he couldn't see his own feet.

"Get the fuck off me!" Roen roared.

They tossed him onto the wet sand. "Enjoy your swim, asshole," one of them said, the rest laughing. They quickly disappeared back into the forest. "Oh, and watch out for the maids. They have sharp teeth," one called out from a distance.

Roen stood and dusted the wet sand from his bare chest. *Fuck.* He needed to find Liv but had no idea where she was. Even if he knew, it was pitch black, the stars and moon covered in a thick blanket of clouds. He didn't have a flashlight, weapons, or—

"Goddammit!" he yelled.

Suddenly, he heard the faint sound of an animal howling. He looked around, but didn't see anything—not that he expected to. The sound of one howl—maybe it was more of a moan—turned into the sounds of dozens.

Roen froze and turned his head toward something yellow flickering and bobbing in the waves. As his eyes focused, he noticed hundreds of them. *Holy bloody fuck*. They were eyes. Something large, cold, and wet slithered across his foot. *Shit*. He turned and ran into the forest. Branches smacked his face and lashed his arms. He didn't know what the hell those things were, but the men had called them maids.

That's when it hit him. Naylor had called themselves—*I can't say it without feeling crazy*—"mermen." Did that mean they believed those creatures were mermaids?

As Roen ran, his foot caught on a rock and his body hurtled into the darkness, landing on his side and knocking the wind from him.

He lay there for a moment, catching his breath, the thumping sound of his heart pounding inside his ears. *Thump, thump. Thump, thump. Thump, thump.* His heart was so goddamned loud he couldn't hear his own thoughts.

He placed his hand over his chest, wondering if it might explode. *That's not my heart.* The beat inside his chest moved to another rhythm—fast, like a galloping horse. This other sound was like a war drum.

Had Naylor been speaking the truth about the island? Roen didn't know, but the sound beckoned him to fight for Liv, to shed blood. Yes, he wanted to kill something. In particular, those assholes who'd taken her.

"Help! Let me the fuck out of here!"

Roen sat up, wondering if he'd imagined the sound of Liv pleading for her life.

"Fucking let me out!" he heard her scream again.

Roen got up and started running.

CHAPTER SEVEN

Liv was in a goddamned cage barely tall enough for someone five feet in height, let alone five seven. And it certainly wasn't wide enough to lie down—if that was the position she chose to be in, which she did not. Because lying across cold rusty bars wasn't something any human being chose. Just like she wouldn't choose to wear an all-white, nearly transparent, strapless dress that was really just a long piece of linen cloth wrapped around her body and tied behind her neck. It was a bathing suit cover-up at best.

How she'd gotten there, she could only guess. But the likely answer was that Holden had put something into her IV to knock her out.

How else was he going to give you a sponge bath? She couldn't believe some stranger had touched her entire body while she was unconscious. *That's so wrong I don't even know where to start.*

And no, just because the man was a doctor didn't make it right even if she appeared to be untouched in any sexual sort of way.

These men need to be flogged and hung by the gonads. Every damned one of them. And that went double for the men who'd attacked Roen. Words couldn't describe how afraid she felt for him and how badly she wanted to see him again.

The only good news was she felt better now that she'd had plenty to drink and saline pumped into her body. The bad news? She was in a fucking cage. In the middle of a huge goddamned room that, well, looked like something straight from the Dark Ages or *Lord of the Rings*. The ceiling reached so high it faded into blackness. And the walls, which appeared to be carved from solid rock, sweated with moisture that gathered into narrow channels along the edges of the floor and flowed away from the main entrance—a soaring doorway that looked like it had been hacked with hand tools. The water then gathered in an eerie iridescent green pool at the far end of the room about fifty meters away.

Other than that creepy pond, the only other light came from a large fireplace to her side. But the smoldering logs were no match for the chill inside the vacuous, glorified cavern.

"Let me the fuck out!" she screamed, rattling the rust-coated bars.

She knew no one would come strolling by and say: "Oh dear. Who has locked you in this dastardly cage? Let me free you immediately, milady." But dammit, standing there doing nothing felt just as ridiculous. She'd rather make some noise than be a good little lamb marching to slaughter.

After twenty minutes or so of screaming, Liv crouched down to rest her back. She let her head fall forward and closed her eyes, trying to think of something—anything—positive. She couldn't let go of hope. That would be the true nail in her coffin.

You have so much to live for, Liv, so much to fight for.

An image of her little sister, Dana, popped inside her head. Dana was only five years younger, but once Dana reached her later teens, people said they looked like twins. Liv, however, still remembered the first time she held her sister—her very own, living baby doll. At least, that was what she'd thought at the time. The tiny fingers and toes and those pink little lips were so precious, exactly like the doll she'd gotten for Christmas, only way better. This one yawned and blinked at her with big eyes. This one felt so warm in her arms. As they grew older, Liv did more and more of the helping, eventually the sitting too. In some ways, it was their relationship that eventually sparked Liv's interest in her field of study. Human connections. Bonds. Love. All that stuff. Dana was like this little anchor of light in her heart, and Liv wondered why. Why did she love one person above another? It wasn't that she didn't love the others in her family or her friends, but Dana was special. She always would be.

"Liv!"

She swiveled her head toward the gaping doorway that led outside into the dark night.

Standing there, wearing only a red cloth tied around his waist, was Roen. His hard rippling abs and chiseled chest glistened with sweat. His arms swelled with ropes of hard muscle and his thighs were no different. *Holy crap.* She'd never seen a more sinfully beautiful, menacing-looking man.

Gripping the bars of her cage, she swallowed the lusty lump in her throat. "Roen?" she croaked. "You're all right?" Of course, that was a stupid question. The man was better than all right.

He stared with a fierce, possessive look in his eyes that sent her heart racing. As surprising as it was, she liked him looking that way at her.

"Did they touch you?" he growled.

"No. Ohmygod, I thought you were dead."

His green and hazel eyes maintained their intense gaze for several moments. Then he flashed a smile that made her heart do a little flip. "Not today."

Liv couldn't believe how good he looked. Whole. Healthy. Strong. And his skin had a golden sheen like he'd been out sunbathing. The last time she'd seen him, he looked like a bloody corpse. "They gave you their water, didn't they?"

He quickly moved to the cage door and began forcefully tugging on the rusty lock. "Yeah. I'm fairly certain that whatever's in it makes them insane." He blew out another breath. "I can't open this—did you see who has the key or where they might've put it?"

"No." She shook her head frantically. "I just woke up in here. Please, you have to get me out. They're going to raffle me off or something."

"No. They're not going to give you away. They're going to perform some gladiator-bullshit-fight-to-the-death ritual to determine who you belong to."

Fight to the death?

"They can't do this," she seethed.

"They can and they will. Are you sure you didn't see anything? A place they might've hidden the key?"

"No. Isn't there something you can use to pick the lock?"

"I'm not a locksmith. I run a freighter company. I read P and Ls and invest money."

Funny, he looked like one of them now. Not some high-profile, wealthy businessman.

"Please, Roen, do something," she pleaded frantically.

His slightly full lips parted as if he were about to speak, but then he pushed them together. Liv was an expert of human observation. She'd logged over a thousand hours of watching people—their facial expressions, body language, changes in skin tone, and breathing patterns. If she were going to take a stab, she'd guess he was a man who was about to lose it. The pulse ticked away on his neck, the cords of muscles—damn, he had a lot of them—were stretched like tight rubber bands about to snap, and his eyes were sort of vacant, like an animal about to kill something.

"Are you okay?" she asked.

He ran his strong hand through his short caramel brown hair and glanced at his bare feet. Yes, they were really, really nice feet. But this was not the time to be drooling over him despite the fact that every inch of him appeared to be perfect.

"No. I'm not foking okay," he seethed. "These people are crazy, Liv. And I don't mean a little weird or eccentric. They think this island is alive."

"Alive. You're joking."

He shot her a look.

Oh God.

"That's not all," he said, his nostrils flaring and his chest heaving. "They think they're mermen."

"Mer. Men?" Liv wasn't sure if she'd heard him correctly. "You mean…men who are half fish?" she asked.

Roen nodded while his eyes scanned the room. She assumed he was looking for something—anything to break the lock.

There was nothing. She'd been checking out the room for over an hour. And now she didn't know if she wanted to laugh or cry with this new bit of information. "These big, overgrown sacks of shit think they're fish?"

"No. They think they're descendants of some group of animals who crawled from the sea and eventually evolved into people. Only they say they're not people."

Liv knew her jaw was hanging open because she wanted to speak, but there were no words for the insanity she'd just heard.

Oh, God. This just keeps getting worse. "They told you this?"

"Yes. I spoke to one of them."

"You. Have. To get. Me out. Of here." She rattled the cage door.

There was a loud noise outside—men laughing and howling.

Roen looked at Liv with hard eyes. "If these people haven't destroyed my phone, there can't be more than a few minutes left on the battery."

Her eyes teared up. "What are you saying?"

He rubbed his face, trying to hammer something out. "My crews are trained to follow strict protocol. When someone goes missing off one of my ships, they are to alert search and rescue. After twelve hours, they are to continue on course."

"What does that mean, Roen?" she hissed, white knuckling the bars.

"It means that even if I got you out, there's no point in running if there's no one to get us off this island."

No. No. No. "You're going to leave me in this cage, aren't you? You're going to let them kill me. That healer man said they kill women." Her words flowed in frantic desperation. "Haven't you noticed, Roen? There are no women on this island! Not one! They sacrifice us or something. You can't leave me here. You can't!"

Roen held up his hand. "I'm not going to let them hurt you. Remember, you belong to me."

She expected him to smile or indicate somehow he was joking, but he didn't. And once again, Liv found herself wondering why the thought of belonging to him made her heart race so fast.

"What are you going to do?"

Roen squared his bare, broad shoulders and headed for the door.

"Roen!" She rattled the door, but he disappeared. Liv sank down, covering her face. This was madness. Pure madness. How could Roen just leave her like this? Was he going to look for a weapon or something? Because there wasn't time.

Please, God. Please help me. God had never listened to her before. Nor had she to God. Hell, she didn't even know if he or she existed. To her, God had always been just another word for the invisible energy that every particle in the universe contained, but miraculously produced everything we ate, touched, and felt—even love. She'd always felt intrigued by that. How can so much come from nothing? But right now, she prayed there was something bigger out there, because she needed help, and she wanted to live. She wanted to see her sisters again. And she'd give anything to watch her parents dancing at their fortieth wedding anniversary just a few months away. The entire family would be there, and Liv was supposed to give the speech. But if she didn't make it through this, there would be no speech. No giant party— something her mother had been looking forward to for months. No celebration.

Just a funeral without a body. The thought of putting them through that broke her heart. She promised whoever—whatever was listening that she'd do something to repay the favor if she got out of this in one piece.

She felt a hard pinch on her arm and yelped. When she looked, there was no one there. Not a soul. *This place is frigging creepy as hell.*

CHAPTER EIGHT

From the confines of her narrow rusty cage, Liv stared at the twenty savage-looking strangers who filed inside the dank, dark, cavernous room and stripped away what little clothing they wore. Some were covered from the waist down, excluding their genitals—thank God—with those strange tribal fish-scale tattoos. Others had images of fierce sea creatures with claws and sharp teeth that snaked around their arms and legs or up their backs and chests. Some had nothing but lots of golden brown skin and huge—she gulped—everything. Well, they all had huge everythings, actually.

But now, given what she'd seen—culturally speaking, of course—and what Roen had told her, coupled with what she knew of tribal societies, these men fell more into the cult category. They were modern men who came to this island and believed it was some sort of god. Perhaps they believed it gave them powers, too, in exchange for ritual sacrifices and sexual acts. The possibility also existed that their water contained a potent concoction of some type of naturally occurring steroid and/or hallucinogenic, which would explain their enormous sizes and mass delusions.

Liv. Seriously? Does any of that matter right now? Because you're about to watch them fight to the death. Naked. For you. She didn't want to witness anyone dying, and certainly not for her. Afterwards, the nightmare would turn into a living hell because she was the prize, and God only knew what the winner would do to her. This wasn't just frightening, it was ludicrous.

"Wait!" she screamed. "Just let me leave. Please!" Yet the men paid her zero attention, forming a line while a few hundred more men, equal in behemoth size, gathered around in a wide circle.

Liv cupped her hands over her face. *I can't believe this is happening. I can't believe this is happening.* She rattled the cage door once again. "Let me the fuck go!" she screamed.

"Is there anyone else who wishes to place a claim on the female?" echoed a voice from somewhere inside the room. "Last call, gentlemen. L'isle will be here any moment to open the claiming, and she's the only female any of us will see until the Collection."

The room fell into an eerie silence.

"All right," said the man. "Then let the claiming be—"

"I place my claim on her," said a cold, confident voice that filled the entire room.

The man pushed his way through the crowd of nearly naked onlookers, who all wore either red or black cloth.

Roen. What the hell?

"No, Roen!" Liv yelled. "Don't!"

One of the men laughed. "You? You wish to fight for the female?"

Roen pushed his way to the center of the room where she could see him, where everyone could see him. Had he lost his frigging marbles?

Roen slowly turned his body, making a circle, staring the men in the eyes. "Yes. But I won't challenge these pieces of shit for her." He then grinned with a sinister twitch in his lips that sent a spike of icy dread through Liv's veins. *Oh no. Oh no. What's he going to do?*

"Oh, really?" one of the men said. "Do you plan to just walk away with her?"

"I plan to challenge your leader." Roen didn't blink. "For control of the island."

Liv gasped. *This* was Roen's plan? For Christ's sake, this wasn't a hostile takeover of another shipping company. His money and stock options were no good here.

Roen was mad. Completely out of his billionaire head if he thought he could fight and win against the barbarian who would be their leader. Yes, Roen was large—about six and a half feet tall with lean, hard muscle—and growing larger since she first laid eyes on him this morning, but his domesticated physique was likely the result of a gym membership and personal trainer.

"Roen! No!" All Liv could think about was how she'd almost watched him die once today, and how badly she wanted him to live. In the short amount of time they'd known each other, she felt something for him that she hadn't ever felt with anyone. It was weird and inexplicable, but who the hell cared? It was what it was. "Run, Roen. Just run!"

"What is this I hear?" said a booming voice near the doorway. Liv's backbone tightened with fear, and the room's temperature dropped ten degrees.

The sea of stone-cold-faced, shirtless men made a path for their leader as he passed. And holy shit. The man—with long brown hair and a beard to match, wearing nothing more than a suede skin around his waist—was at least a head taller than all the rest. Scars covered his tanned skin, and every inch of him flexed with rhino-sized muscles. He looked like the Grim Reaper masquerading in Conan the Barbarian's skin. His fitness plan was probably killing people. Big people. Who disobeyed him.

Roen is going to die. I'm going to die.

"Did I hear someone wishes to challenge me?" From the edge of the circle surrounding Liv and the twenty naked men, their leader's fiercely intimidating gaze swept the room.

Roen, who stared at the man, looked like he just might faint. Then, like he'd gotten over the shock, his disposition completely shifted. Legs apart, arms crossed, a defiant crazed look in his eyes.

No, Roen. Don't do it. Just shut up. She prayed he'd come to his senses now that he'd seen the man he'd just challenged to a fight.

Roen stepped toward the leader, his neck and jaw pulsing with powerful, tense muscles. Something about Roen reminded her of a shark. A hungry great white shark with cold, soulless eyes.

Oh shit. He's really going to do this.

The leader laughed and stepped forward, placing them several feet apart. "I haven't torn off anyone's head today, so I accept, little man. And I choose fists."

Roen cracked his neck, his green eyes shimmering with a wicked death wish. "I wouldn't have it any other way, brother."

Brother? Had Roen meant that literally or figuratively?

"Please don't, Roen," Liv pleaded. "I'm not worth it." She was worth it, but Roen dying for her wasn't right. It wasn't what she wanted.

Roen glanced at Liv. "Don't forget what I told you, Liv. You're mine."

৵৽

When Roen came to the obvious conclusion that his odds were significantly better challenging one man versus twenty, he still knew it was a huge risk. But what other options did he have? Walk away? Stay and watch? No. For whatever reason, this strange woman had gotten under his skin. And despite his inability to explain it, it was pointless pretending otherwise. He was in this now, and it was up to him to see this through to the bitter end—probably his bitter end.

Only now, there was a whole new issue. One that shook him so hard, he could've sworn his teeth had clacked.

Roen had expected someone tough, someone large to be these men's leader. But Roen had not expected this: Lyle. His little brother, who'd supposedly died over fifteen years ago.

How had he gotten here?

Roen didn't know. But Lyle didn't seem to recognize him. And it wasn't because Roen had changed. It was because something had clearly been done to Lyle, and Roen wasn't referring to the fact that Lyle had grown a foot taller or put on a hundred bleedin' pounds of muscle. The Lyle he knew growing up hated fighting, and he'd certainly never threaten to kill someone.

What am I going to do? Roen thought while trying to block out the sound of that goddamned war drum thumping away in the back of his mind, telling him how much he wanted Liv, how much he wanted to kill for her.

"You have some big balls to call me 'brother,'" said Lyle. "Let's see what words come from your mouth when I'm ripping out your tongue."

Oh hell. Roen needed to win this fight, but killing his brother?

He needed a moment to think.

Roen cracked his neck again and grinned. "I meant brother as a term of endearment. Just as one might refer to their dog."

A low rumble of chuckles erupted from the crowd. Lyle's large chest shook with laughter. "I'm going to enjoy killing you, landlover."

Roen dipped his head. "And if I win?"

Lyle raised his brows. "You? Win? Not likely. But if you would like to indulge us with your terms, we're all ears."

"If I win, the woman is mine and she goes home."

The man flicked his thick wrist. "If you win, you'll be the new leader and she is yours to claim and do with as you please—within the laws of the island, of course. But I wouldn't count my chickens yet, little man. The island hasn't asked me to step down."

"Roen!" he heard Liv call out, but paid no attention. He couldn't afford to be distracted. And the way she looked, freshly scrubbed body and wrapped up in white like a giant fuckable present, was a definite distraction.

Roen stepped in closer. "That's because the island asked *me* to take you down."

Lyle jerked back his head. "The island has spoken to you?"

It was a bluff, of course, but Roen knew that winning a fight always started with the mind—your own and your opponent's.

He's not your opponent. He's your brother. And that meant the only way to truly win was to get Lyle to back down or back down himself.

You think they'll let you walk away now? You've thrown out a challenge. Then what's going to happen to Liv? There had to be a way out of this.

Roen nodded. "How the hell do you think I got here?"

"Like everyone else."

"Yes, but not everyone who comes is a Doran. Not everyone here has a right to lead."

"And so you are right," Lyle said, removing the suede wrapped around his waist. "Shall we?"

The men stepped back and waited for Roen to remove the red sash.

"Can I ask one question before we begin?" Roen asked.

Lyle laughed with a smug chuckle. "Of course. I am in a generous mood and would like nothing more than to grant your dying wish."

The men around him roared with laughter.

"Do you know who you are—who you once were?"

"L'isle. I am called L'isle. Son of Cullan, same as you, Roen."

Roen blinked. Cullan was his father's name. "So you know I'm your brother?"

"These men," his arms made a sweeping motion, "are my brothers. You are the useless, landlover offspring of my father."

Roen felt a surge of unfathomable conflict. Lyle did remember him. But there was absolutely no way

Lyle would ever want to fight him. Their relationship couldn't have been any closer.

How close could you have been if Lyle let you believe he'd committed suicide? They'd never found the body, but the note said it all: he couldn't be happy living like this anymore. Witnesses said they'd seen him jump into the ocean.

Roen suddenly felt a deep-seated rage. All these years he'd suffered from the loss of his brother. All these years. And here he was alive. Everything Roen had done—getting Lyle out of foster care once he turned eighteen, working two shitty jobs to support them both after their mom died, making sure Lyle had a safe home away from their father—none of that meant anything to Lyle. He'd just left and let Roen think he'd killed himself.

Why would he do this to me? Why would Lyle—

Lyle lunged and knocked Roen across the room, sending him hurtling into the damp stone walls. Roen felt his newly healed ribs crack on impact.

He fell to the floor, seeing a black cloud with flecks of bright light. Meanwhile, Liv's cries echoed somewhere in the background of his mind. They were the same cries he'd heard earlier in the day when they'd beaten him within an inch of his life.

In that moment, lying there on the floor in agony, he realized that was why his feelings for Liv had so drastically changed. Earlier, she had attacked one of the men in an attempt to protect him. Him. A complete bastard who'd stopped doing anything for anyone after the loss of his brother. But Liv's gesture had triggered something deep inside him. *She* had triggered something deep inside him.

The room filled with roars and cheering. *Get up, Roen. Get the foke up.* Shoving aside his screaming pain, Roen staggered to his feet and braced his hands on his knees.

Lyle threw out his arms and shook his head. "The landlover wants more, gentlemen," he bellowed. "Shall I give it to him?"

The men cheered with raised fists.

"As you wish!" Lyle yelled with a gloating smile.

Roen managed to stand straight just as Lyle rushed forward. With one hand, Lyle slammed him against the wall by the neck while delivering a blow to his stomach. Pain shot through every inch of Roen's body, and he slid down to the floor, unable to breathe.

As Roen lay there in a daze, his mind shuffled through random memories—being hit over and over again by the guys in the group home, kicking in his nose. The boys at his school near Glasgow when he was nine, throwing rocks at him in retribution for what his father had done to their families' fishing boats. Sunken. Still, those bumps and bruises were nothing compared to what they'd done to Lyle. No eight-year-old should have to pay for his father's sins, but Lyle paid. He'd spent fourteen weeks in the hospital having his face reconstructed and healing from the cuts all over his body. Was that enough to get his father to stop?

No. It was just the beginning. It fueled his father's hatred and justified hurting more people.

But that was the past, and this was a fight Roen couldn't lose. Whatever choices Lyle had made, whatever had been done to him, he was no longer the same person. Then there was Liv. Innocent in all this.

Accept the island. Accept, and you'll win. Roen's mind jolted. He didn't know where the thought originated, but it didn't matter. He did not want to die. He did not want to let them take Liv.

Accept the island. Accept, and you'll win, the voice repeated.

I accept. Roen then noticed a cool trickle of water running over his lips, which were partially pressed to the floor. He swallowed and gulped, every drop strengthening him, healing him.

"Get up, landlover! Come, take your throne," Lyle yelled, his laughter filling the room.

Roen slowly pushed himself to his hands and knees. He could hear the heavy footsteps approaching, see that leg pulling back, readying to deliver a blow. Roen reached out and grabbed Lyle's foot, twisting with so much force, he felt the ankle snap like a branch. A loud cry echoed through the cavernous room as Lyle crashed to the floor.

Roen leaped on top of him and began punching Lyle in the face. With each strike of his fist, more and more blood poured from Lyle's nose, fueling Roen's rage. "Are you laughing now? Think you can break someone like me?" Roen cocked his fist, ready to strike the fatal blow to Lyle's throat and crush his windpipe.

Lyle looked into his eyes. "Dorans can't be broken."

That was what Roen used to tell Lyle every goddamned day: "They can't break you, Lyle. Because no one can break a Doran's spirit. It's stronger than any fist," he'd say.

What the hell am I doing? The urge to kill Lyle was overwhelming, like some sort of primal craving.

"Don't make me do this," Roen seethed.

The men around him began chanting, "Kill him. Kill him."

"Do it," Lyle said.

Roen raised his fist higher and looked into his brother's eyes. They hadn't changed. Same color— green with a ring of amber flecks in the middle, just like his.

Foke. I can't.

Roen dropped his fist. "The island told me to let you live if you surrender."

Lyle stared blankly. "The rules state that one must die."

Roen shrugged. "Who am I to question the island? It says it's not done with you yet." He honestly couldn't understand how anyone would buy his reasoning, but they were all mad. They might believe anything.

"Do you surrender?" Roen yelled. *Please, Lyle. Don't make me kill you.*

Lyle slowly nodded and held up his hands. "I surrender, as the island wills it to be."

Roen dropped his fist and hopped up, his eyes sweeping the room. The faces of the large, savage men were that of utter disbelief. Roen immediately understood that he'd just won the battle, but not the war. He'd need to establish his authority or else he'd find himself being dragged outside and slaughtered.

This is no different from the dozens of hostile takeovers you've orchestrated. Once the leader was out, people needed to understand their lives were hitched to a new wagon. Of course, his wagon usually wore a suit and tie, not a scrap of red cloth around his waist. Not to mention, in this case, speeches or memos wouldn't do. Roen would have to make an example of someone.

Roen looked around the room and spotted the largest man, who happened to be the same guy with long dark hair that had nearly killed him earlier that day. "You. What's your name again?"

"Shane," he replied.

"Shane, apologize to the lady for your behavior earlier, and then get her the foke out of that cage."

Shane didn't move.

"Do it," Roen commanded in a final warning, hoping his bluff wouldn't be called, but there it was. No other choice. "Or better yet, don't. Because I'd love nothing more than to kill you. And for the record, the island has not instructed me to spare you. You are *not* my brother. Not until you prove yourself."

With a stiff spine, the man walked to the cage and looked down at Liv. "I apologize for the way I treated you earlier," he said between gritted teeth.

Liv, who looked like she might faint and was at the end of her mental ropes, didn't say a word.

"Good," Roen said. "Now let her out and get inside the cage. You'll stay there until I say so."

Shane glanced at one of the men, who scrambled over and handed him a key. He opened the cage, and Liv cautiously moved around him. Shane got inside, hunching to make himself fit.

Roen walked over and took Liv's hand, stopping to address the room. "This woman is mine. Anyone so much as lays a damned finger on her, they'll die."

No one made eye contact.

Roen then pointed to Lyle. "I'll be back later, and then you and I are going to talk. As for the rest of you, get your asses back to...whatever it is you do around here."

He strode from the room as quickly as his feet could carry him, with Liv in tow.

CHAPTER NINE

"Roen? Where the hell are we going?" Liv's breath steamed into the cold night air as she tried to keep up. He moved so fast with his long legs that she had to do double time. Despite feeling better, she still wasn't at one hundred percent. More like sixty.

"As far away as we can get from those men," he said.

"I can't believe that just happened. Who the hell was that guy, Roen?"

"My brother."

"How did he end up here?" she asked, assuming that perhaps this was what Roen had come here looking for.

"I don't know." He continued marching at a vigorous pace.

"Roen, stop for a second and talk to me."

"We need to keep moving."

Well, she needed to make sure her head didn't explode. What happened back there was…was…chaos! *Roen is the leader of an island full of woman killers.*

"Roen," she argued, "you said there's nowhere to run—your ship is gone. So where are we going?"

"I already told you. Away from them." He grabbed her hand and pulled her along.

She tried to take her hand back, but he tightened his grip, nearly crushing her bones. "Stop! You're hurting me."

Roen did stop. "Sorry. I don't know what's happening to me. I think I'm losing my mind."

Except for a haze of moonlight filtering through the tree canopy, there wasn't much light. But what Liv saw of his face was absolute turmoil.

"Roen, what's going on with you?" she whispered. Yeah, she knew everything was in a state of pandemonium, but she could see there was something else.

"I don't know."

"Yes, you do."

"Why do you care, Ms. Stratton?"

She wanted to punch him. "Did you just call me 'Ms.'? Like we're in a business meeting? Uh-uh. I think we're past the formal stage." The guy had just laid his life on the line for her.

"Foke." He gripped the sides of his head. "I need to get you off this island."

"Correction—*we* need to get off this island." She grabbed one of his arms and instantly noticed how hot he felt. "What did they do to you?"

"I don't know. I think it's that damned water."

"How much did you drink?"

"Enough."

Okay. That was not good. "How do you feel?" she asked, her teeth beginning to chatter. With every passing moment, the air became colder and colder. All she had on was a glorified bed sheet.

He blew out a steaming breath. "I've been better."

"But you're okay. I mean, you're still you?"

"Who the hell else would I be?" he snapped.

Yep. Bigger and sexier—if that's even possible— but still an ass. It was a relief. On the other hand, she was genuinely worried about him. He'd taken not just one, but two beatings for her.

"What you did back there was—" *All right. There are no words.* "Thank you, Roen. I don't know what I would've done if you hadn't pulled that stunt, but... What the hell were you *thinking*?" she yelled, the emotional safety valve blowing clean off. "I mean... Goddammit, Roen! You could've been killed. And for what? For me? Did you ever consider that I wouldn't want to live if it was at your expense? Did you?"

"You're welcome," he retorted. "But I didn't do it for you."

"Then for who?"

Suddenly, Roen grabbed her upper arms and slammed her against a thick tree. His mouth was on her, his hard body pinning her every curve against him.

Liv felt too shocked to do anything but stand there stiff as a board. Roen was equally stiff, but below the waist. His lips smashed into hers, his tongue forcefully delved into her mouth, and he ground himself against her. Liv's mind went into panic mode, wondering if this wasn't truly Roen, but some reaction—perhaps to the fight and elevated testosterone, to the situation, to the water. Not that the "why" mattered. Because when his hands slid down the sides of her body, raking over her breasts as he went to cup her ass, Liv realized how badly she'd been wanting this. Maybe from the first moment she'd laid eyes on him. No, she didn't want him to stop. She wanted him to touch her. She wanted to lose herself in him, to bathe her senses in every inch of his hard body.

She turned her head to free her mouth, and he turned his attention to her neck—kissing, sucking, scraping with his teeth.

"God, you feel so good," she panted. And his smell... It was like heaven—sweet and spicy, calming yet stimulating.

"I want to fuck you, Liv," he said, in a carnal, gravelly tone, lifting her up as if she weighed nothing.

"Roen..." Her voice trailed off into a soft moan as Roen ground his rigid shaft between her legs, igniting a sinful heat that crippled all rational thought. Suddenly there was just her and him and that erotic ache deep inside, pulsing and throbbing, begging for him to penetrate her.

She dug her nails into the hard, straining muscles of his shoulders, wincing with sinful pleasure each time he crushed his large cock against her. His hands moved beneath the fabric of her makeshift dress and began sliding it up. "You want me to fuck you. Isn't that right, Liv?"

Roen sliding inside her, fucking her hard, and coming between her thighs was the only thing she wanted. *What's happening to me?* It wasn't like her to want something like that—so reckless. But she did. Perhaps the island was changing her, too.

"Yes," she panted. And when she thought about the way he'd fearlessly stood up to those crazy men to save her, it only made her want him more. The man was a complete enigma and sexy as hell.

Kissing her neck, he reached between them and tugged at the red cloth around his waist to free his erection. "You're mine. I fought for you. You're mine."

"Yes." She turned her head into his neck, feverishly kissing and licking him back. She couldn't get enough of his touch and skin and smell. "Yes, I'm yours." She tightened the grip with her legs around his waist, ready for his hard thrust.

"That's right. Mine." Gripping himself in his hand, he positioned his shaft at her entrance and made a few teasing circles with the head before testing her readiness with a shallow thrust.

Liv gasped. Even with just the tip, Liv felt her body struggling to accept the thickness. And then she felt something else: his teeth.

Roen bit down on her shoulder, and she screamed. Roen released her and stumbled back.

"What the hell was that?" She felt like she'd been splashed with a bucket of ice-cold water. And though it was dark and she couldn't clearly see his face, she knew his expression was the same as hers.

"Why did you bite me?" she raged.

A silent moment passed. "I don't know," he said with a shaken voice, "but you have to get out of here. You have to get away from me."

Something strange was happening to him—to them both, perhaps. Yet, he was still her only lifeline, and he was too good of a person to be left to these sea-wolves. "I'm not leaving you."

"I'm infected, Liv. Whatever they have, it's in me now." Roen dipped down and grabbed his...whatever the hell they called their little man-skirts.

"Then we need to get you to a hospital." The water had to contain some sort of neurotoxin. Or maybe it was a new PCP-like narcotic that gave a person superhuman strength.

"Liv, you've seen the men on this island. You've seen what that water does. There are no drugs that heal people from broken bones in a matter of minutes. Whatever that crap is, it's changing me. I'm getting you the hell out of here. Away from me. Away from them."

This was all her fault. He probably could've left the island if it weren't for her. But instead, Roen stepped in to help her—three times. And now the man was their damned leader. Leader! *How the hell did this happen?*

She moved and stood directly in front of him, trying to see his face and hoping he could see the look on hers. "I told you; I'm not leaving you with these animals."

"You can send help once you're somewhere safe."

"Roen, no—"

"I'm not asking," he said in a cold, deep voice. "It's a matter of time before I end up like Lyle—brainwashed and violent."

"You mean your brother?"

"My dead brother. Somehow he ended up here. Alive, twelve inches taller, and a hundred pounds heavier."

"He died?" she asked, hoping to hell that Roen didn't mean he died for real. That would be a whole other kind of crazy. Seriously, seriously, bad-scary crazy.

"Apparently not."

Oh, thank God.

"Maybe he can help us, Roen. He can tell us how to get home."

"Are you hearing yourself? You just said our best hope is my brother—a person who has been leading these deranged thugs for God only knows how long and just tried to kill me."

"I don't see a better option, do you?" she said.

"No." He shot out a frustrated sigh. "I actually don't. But I'm going to see him alone."

Liv gripped his arm. "Uh-uh. We stick together."

"I can't have you around a pack of crazy arses who think they're part fish. I can't risk anyone hurting you."

"Then you and I feel the same; neither wants to see the other hurt."

And there it was: that...*something*. That invisible force that bonded two people. It was like gravity, holding one object to another. But in the case of people, there were no mathematical formulas to explain the ties that formed between them. Parents and children. Brothers and sisters. Friends and lovers. It was real. It could make or break a person. It could bring a profound sense of joy and fulfillment or leave a person devastated when lost. Yet there was no tangible, scientific proof to support the physical existence of these connections. Yes, people understood the emotional impact when a bond with another person formed or broke. But it escaped her how something so important and central to every human being on the planet couldn't be seen. Something connected people. Something real. And it allowed them to form these powerful attachments. *So powerful that one might give their life for the other.* And now one of those bonds had formed with Roen—a man she met less than a day ago. She felt like she might never breathe again if she lost him.

The two stared at each other for several long moments, unable to truly see one another, but Liv had the distinct impression that Roen struggled with the same inexplicable emotions.

"You have no idea what I'm feeling," he said bitterly, responding to her last comment.

"Try explaining it, then."

"I can't. I simply know I can no longer be trusted around you. The things I just felt—they were not the thoughts of a sane man. They were not…me."

"That's ridiculous, Roen. You're letting this place get to you."

"No!" he burst out, reaching for her shoulders to give her a good shake. "I won't. Go to fucking hell."

Huh? It took a moment to get past the shock of this incredibly strong man painfully gripping her shoulders, to realize that Roen was not talking to her.

"Roen. Stop!"

He released her and once again gripped the sides of his head, groaning. "I won't do it!" he yelled.

Ohmygod. She needed to get him to a doctor. Maybe that water *was* poison. But then again, she'd had the same water, and she wasn't hearing voices.

"Roen, take a deep breath." She reached for his shoulders to comfort him.

He ground out his words. "You have to go, Liv."

"You're a good man," she said softly, "and just like I don't deserve to be left here; you don't deserve that either. We. Are in this. Together."

Roen took several deep breaths and finally dropped his hands. A patch of moonlight illuminated his strikingly handsome face, his lightly stubbled jawline catching the light.

"You're all right now. See," she said with a calming voice. "Try to breathe."

He nodded and then shoved his hands through his hair. "I was born in Scotland."

"Okay." Why had he said that?

"I lived there until I was ten when we fled from my father. He was one of them—the men from this island. He was violent and cruel—not with us, but with everyone else."

Liv shook her head. "I-I don't understand."

"It's what defines everything about me. Everything, right down to the fact I refuse to sound like him. So I'll be damned if I end up ruining a good woman's life."

"You think you're ruining my life?" *He just saved it!*

"Liv," he said quietly, his tone dead serious, "I'm getting you off this island, but I'm not going with you."

"What? *Why?*" she snapped.

"I need to help Lyle."

The person who'd just tried to kill him? "That's bullshit."

"Is it? If it was your sister—what was her name? Dana? Would you leave her here?"

"Okay. No. I wouldn't. So we all leave together," Liv said. "I'm not afraid."

Roen stepped toward her. "You should be. Just like I should be claiming you."

Suddenly, the air between them thickened again.

Oh no! She shoved out her hands, but it did no good. He suddenly had her by the shoulders again, gripping her firmly with his shaking hands as if he wanted to maul her.

She reached out and slapped him across the cheek. "Roen!"

He let her go and drove his fist right into the tree behind her.

My God. He is losing it. Maybe he was right; she needed to get away from this place and return with help. But leaving him behind? She just didn't want to do that. Her other option was to wait until his ship came back for them. She'd do everything in her power to make sure Roen left, too.

"I'll leave the island," she said. *But you're coming with me whether you like it or not.*

"I'm glad you see things my way. My ship is probably gone, but if I can get to my phone, I can call the crew. They'll turn around and come back. I just hope that my cell still has power. Otherwise, I'll see what Lyle or the other men can tell me about transportation. They have to have some way of getting on and off the island."

"Roen, the healer guy, Holden, has satellite TV."

"He has dish TV?"

"He also has state-of-the-art medical equipment—respirators, heart monitors, CT scanner…" That other guy, Shane, had French windows. She doubted they were making glass on the island. That meant they were definitely importing stuff, which meant they had some means of contacting the outside.

"Then they have electricity and might have other electronics, too. Maybe even their own satellite cell, which they will give to me since I'm now their leader. As for you, we're going to find a place to hide you until I've made contact with my ship."

"What about food and water?" she asked.

"I'll come back at daybreak with supplies." Roen grabbed her hand and pulled her along, continuing toward the other side of the island without saying a word. His palm felt hot and buzzed with a weird energy. Not uncomfortable, but powerful enough for her to know it wasn't her imagination.

Whatever was happening to the man, it was real.

"Liv, before I forget. Stay away from the water at night. There are monsters."

CHAPTER TEN

Unlike herself, Roen seemed to have no issues navigating in the dark over rocks and through thick vegetation. She suspected that whatever changes were occurring inside him, improved night vision was one of them. She didn't want to ask. Didn't want to know. The idea of him transforming into something else terrified her. But, of course, that was outrageous. People didn't transform. And those men could believe anything they liked, but calling themselves "mermen" was indisputably the most ridiculous thing she'd ever heard.

God, none of this makes any sense. But that didn't matter. Survival did.

The two hiked in silence, away from that strange mountain where the men had held her prisoner, but it didn't take long before she and Roen ran out of land.

"What next?" Liv asked, the sound of crashing waves behind her. They hadn't found anywhere even remotely safe for her to camp out for a day. It seemed the island was nothing but beach, forest and one giant mountain smack in the middle.

Roen was quiet for several moments. "I was hoping for some sort of high ground where you can see people coming before they see you, but this will have to do."

The temperature was far warmer compared to inland, but it didn't seem hidden enough.

"It's secluded and out of the way," he added. "You'll be shielded from the wind. I don't think it'll get much better than this."

Perhaps he was right. Truth was that the island—maybe three miles wide in each direction by her estimation—was much too small for anyone to hide. At best, she'd avoid being seen for a few days by staying on her guard.

That said, "You told me I should stay away from the water." Both Roen and Shane believed there were monsters—*ridiculous!*—but she could believe a few dangerous animals called this eerie mess of an island their home.

"I don't hear those *things*," Roen replied, "but if you do, you run inland."

"What if I don't hear them?"

"Trust me, you will."

Liv officially had cold feet. "Roen, you seem okay now, so—"

"No, Liv. You have no clue what's going on inside my head. I'm hanging on by a thread." He reached for her hand and gave it a squeeze. "I promise I'll be back soon with food and water." He then placed a gentle kiss on the top of her hand, his lips lingering for several long moments. Liv immediately began to feel that...that—whatever— odd tension filling the air. God, she wanted to kiss him and wrap her arms around him and smell his skin, just one last time.

"I have to go," he said, dropping her hand.

She sucked in a breath and held on for a long moment before exhaling. "I know."

"I'll be back. I promise."

She nodded, but didn't speak, and Roen disappeared into the forest, back toward that mountain. She prayed like hell nothing would happen to him. On this island, however, the chances of that were slim.

⋙⋘

Roen hadn't been separated from Liv for more than five minutes before those gnawing primal urges to go back and take her hard started up again. At first, Roen did his best to push them away, but the more he fought, the more insistent the need became.

"I won't do it," he growled, unsure of who he really spoke to.

"You'll do what I say, or she will be punished," said a feminine voice.

Roen halted in his tracks, his eyes darting from side to side. Had he really heard that, or was he imagining it? "Hello?"

"Hello, Roen. I'm looking forward to our time together."

"Who the hell is this?"

"My dear, sweet merman," she said, *"I think you know the answer to that. But take comfort; your sacrifices will not be in vain."*

What the bloody foke was going on?

"What sacrifices?" Roen then felt his body slam into the dirt, his muscles convulsing and burning with unspeakable pain.

"Just relax, my dear, strong man, and it will soon be over."

Roen screamed in agony, his body bucking as he resisted whatever was trying to take hold. But as the moments passed, the pain subsided, leaving Roen with a clarity of mind he'd never experienced.

Lying there in the dark, Roen drew a deep breath and opened his eyes. Millions of stars shimmered overhead, and a sense of peace washed over him. Suddenly, he felt alive for the first time ever. Then a bright flash hit him. With it he felt and saw years or centuries or millennia of events through the eyes of the island.

"My God," he said. "You really are alive."

"Welcome home, merman."

એવજ

Liv had only been standing on the empty beach, lost in her thoughts and warding off her fear of what might happen if Roen didn't return, for a few short minutes when the sound of shrill voices filled the salty night air. They wailed and howled like ghosts of tortured souls. Then the sound of cracking—like bones crushing—filled the air. The howling stopped and turned into grunting and tearing.

Holy shit. Liv scrambled up the nearest tree, a few yards from the beach, and held her breath. She listened as something—a whole lot of somethings—slithered beneath her through the sand and brush. *Oh shit. Oh shit. Oh shit.* She'd never been so utterly freaked out in her entire life.

After thirty minutes or so, all became quiet, but Liv was not about to go anywhere. She clung to that damned tree through the night just like she clung to her sanity.

In the morning, exhausted from lack of sleep and beginning to once again feel the effects of dehydration, Liv climbed down and found the beach filled with long bloody tracks. *Holy crap.* She couldn't tell what animal had made them, but it looked like a sea lion or something big.

But those animals aren't nocturnal. And they certainly didn't hunt prey on land and drag it into the ocean.

Whatever those "monsters" were, they were something big and dangerous.

The rest of the morning, Liv waited. And waited. But there was no sign of Roen. It was exactly as she feared—they'd separate, something would happen to him, and she'd be left alone, wondering what the hell to do. Then there was the fact that she couldn't stop thinking about the way Roen had grabbed her last night and how his strong hands slid over her breasts, how his hard cock nearly made her explode just from the friction. The man simply touched her, and she felt an undeniable, raw, sexual need for him. Only, he wasn't touching her now, and she felt her body heating up for him all over again, craving the touch of his sensual, full lips on her mouth and neck.

But Roen wasn't only sexy. The connection she felt between them provoked an emotional rush that went far beyond just plain physical attraction. It was impossible to fully explain, except to say that now that they'd met, she found it difficult to imagine her life without him in it. Was it really possible to feel that way about someone she'd only just met?

Yeah. Hellooo. It's possible.

So where the hell was he? *He'll be here. He'll be here.*

But when he didn't show, Liv's hunger and thirst finally got the best of her, and she had no choice but to leave the beach to forage for a few hours. Sadly, however, aside from a few berries, there wasn't much. As for water, she found absolutely nothing.

At the end of the day, when the entire sky lit up with flames of burnt orange and the sun began dipping into the horizon, Liv's panic turned into something much worse. There'd been no sign of Roen all day, and she felt too weak to spend another night in a tree. A few hours, at best, and she'd be passing out, left helpless to whatever animals roamed the night.

Maybe I should head for that mountain and go look for him. There was also water somewhere over there and those things—whatever they were—might not go that far inland. On the other hand, she had no doubt she'd run into one of those men.

Dammit. Just wait it out a little longer. He'll show. He'll show. Please be all right. Truthfully, nothing else really seemed to matter.

But as the sun made its final retreat, Liv knew she'd been wrong. *No Roen.* Her heart sank at the thought of him killed or being beaten again.

I know I'll regret this, but he'd do it for you—

Liv was about to head toward the mountain when howls and groans exploded from the direction of the crashing waves.

Liv darted up that damned tree again, just in time to avoid them. She strained her eyes to see, but they were black, appearing as oblong shadows slinking low across the sand. Dozens of them moved beneath her, and she heard dozens more moving through the thicket.

Holy Christ. What are those things?

Like the night before, thirty minutes later all was quiet again. Liv debated making a run for it. *But to where?* Those things were inland and running on the beach was pointless. Sooner or later, she'd run into them.

Oh God, I'm screwed. And Roen was probably dead. There was simply no other explanation.

The thought sucked the will to fight right out of her. No, she didn't want to die either, but the thought of never seeing Roen again destroyed her. *I can't stay up here; I need to rest and figure this out.* She began climbing down, slowly feeling her way, but on the final branch, her foot slipped. She landed with a thump on the moist, sandy ground below. The wind hadn't been knocked out of her, but falling ten feet still hurt like hell. Then she heard a loud rustle approaching.

No. No. They're coming back. She wanted to scream for help, but what good would it do? No one was coming to save her and making noise would only draw them faster.

The crunch of branches, only ten feet or so from where she lay, made her shake with fear. She slowly got to her feet and began reaching for that first branch. *Shit.* It had snapped. That was why she'd fallen.

Another loud crunch. This time closer. And another.

Oh, God. They're going to tear me to pieces.

"Woman, where the fuck are you?"

Liv saw the shadow of a large man standing a few feet away. No, it wasn't Roen. His voice was different.

"Who are you?" she whispered.

"Forgot me so quickly, landlover?"

Oh shit. It was that Shane guy. "No. That would be impossible."

"Good." He reached for her arm, but she jerked it back and turned to flee. Shane quickly threw her over his shoulder. She couldn't believe this was happening again.

Heart pounding with fear and anger, Liv pushed his neck to gain leverage, but he was incredibly strong. "I belong to Roen," she yelled, hoping to hell that this time that might mean something.

"Yeah, I know. Who do you think sent me?"

"Roen didn't send you." She squirmed and pushed and punched his back.

"Who do you think let me out of the cage?" Shane slapped her hard on the ass. "And stop moving, or I might hurt you for real."

"I bet you'd like that." She managed to get her mouth on a small bit of flesh on his back. He yelled and dropped her.

"What the fuck? You bit me! That's not how things are done around here."

He reached for her, and she held out her arms defensively. "I'm not going anywhere with you."

"Fine. I'll leave you. Hear any strange sounds during the night?"

"Yes. What are they?" she asked.

"I told you: monsters. And they'd love to sink their teeth into something sweet and juicy like you."

Did he think she was eight and that he could frighten her into coming with him? Of course, that didn't mean the animals she'd heard weren't dangerous. "The only monster I've seen is standing right in front of me."

"Me? I'm a pussy cat. Especially compared to those things," he said, half laughing.

"Monsters aren't real."

"Tell that to them. Come on." He yanked her arm and began dragging her along.

"Wait! Just tell me why he didn't come himself."

"He's busy," Shane growled.

Or dead because you crazy bastards killed him. "Okay. But why are *you* running errands for him?"

"He's our leader now, and he'll kill me if I don't obey."

Uh-huh. "You're afraid of Roen." She didn't believe it for a second.

"Isn't everyone?"

"No."

"Then you're an idiot," he replied.

His conviction seemed genuine, but something wasn't right. Roen wouldn't have sent one of these thugs, especially this one, to come for her. He'd know that she wouldn't trust him—Roen had seen this man attack her.

"Where are you taking me?" she panted.

"I thought we covered that; to Roen. Where else would you go?"

"Home."

He laughed. "You're not ready to go home."

She'd expected him to say "never," as in "you're never going home" because they chopped their women up into tiny pieces and fed them to the "monsters."

Liv's mind ran through the options. Those things were out there and would soon be making their way back to the water. She had to go somewhere. And trying to stay awake in a damned tree wasn't going to happen. She hadn't slept at all last night.

"I'll go with you, but I can walk on my own." She'd go with him inland a little ways until she felt sure they'd moved past those things, and then she'd slip away and hide. As soon as the sun came up, she'd start looking for Roen.

"As you wish. Right this way."

Liv did her best to move slowly, conserving her energy, but after ten minutes or so, Shane grumbled under his breath and scooped her up into his arms. "You're the slowest woman on the planet."

"You'll have to excuse me—I must be overwhelmed by the amazing hospitality. Zapped the spunk right out of me."

"Don't be smart with me, woman," he barked.

"You tried to drown me. I think this attitude is as good as it gets."

"I wasn't going to kill you; I was making a point," he retorted.

"You expect me to believe that?"

"If I'd wanted you dead, you wouldn't have seen it coming. Instead, I saved you. I even gave you our sacred water," he said.

Wow. A true gentlemen. "If only your crazy-juice worked on non-mermen," she said facetiously.

"I heard about that."

"About what?" she asked, her voice full of hostility. She hated him touching her.

"That you're resistant to the island."

Oh no. I love it here. More, please. "Yeah. Shocking that I could resist such a paradise."

Shane chuckled. "Our island is better than paradise. Our water cures even the worst injuries. If you're still sick, then there's something wrong with you. Either that, or the island doesn't want you to live."

These people were so primitive in their beliefs. "So what exactly is in your precious water?" she asked bitterly.

"The source of all life."

Pfft. "Ah. Now I see; your water is the fountain of youth."

"No. It can't make you younger. And you won't live forever. It does, however, prolong life."

"Oh reeeally. How old are you?"

"Eighty-two. But I'm a baby compared to some of the others."

He was mad. Totally and completely mad.

"You don't believe me, do you?" he said.

"No."

"You saw Roen. You saw him beaten then perfectly fine a few hours later."

That she had. "Okay. But there has to be some sort of explanation. Maybe he wasn't as hurt as I thou—"

"There is an explanation. I just gave it to you," he said.

"And I suppose you really think you're a fish, too?"

Shane stopped walking. "Don't ever fucking call me that."

"What?"

"We are not fish," he growled.

"Someone told Roen that you call yourselves mermen."

"Yes," he said.

"Aren't mermen half fish?"

"Woman, do you see any scales or gills on me? How about a goddamned tail?"

"No, I don't. But then why do you call yourselves mermen?"

"Our great ancestors were the first humans to crawl from the ocean."

"So your tails just…fell off," she said.

"Something like that."

"Where I come from, there's a name for people like you without tails. They're called human beings."

"No. We are bigger, stronger, smarter. We are not the same as you landlovers."

"You look like men to me," she said.

"We *are* men. Mer. Men."

The conversation had just made a full circle. *Or a crazy granny knot.* "I don't get it, but I don't think I want to."

"You will," he said with a deep ominous tone.

The only thing she'd "get" was the hell away from him. After fifteen minutes, it was time to make her move. This part of the forest seemed denser and darker and there were no signs of those things.

"I need you to stop," she said.

"No. We're already running late."

"For what?" she asked.

"Roen wishes to bed you tonight."

What the fuu…? "Sorry?"

"Bed you," Shane repeated. "He hasn't completed the claiming ceremony."

"What the hell are you talking about?"

"I'll let him explain."

Oh shit. She suddenly wondered which Roen would be waiting for her. The real one? Or the one who seemed to be changing into one of these men?

"You have to stop. I really need to pee."

"No," he barked.

"It will take thirty seconds," she argued. "Thirty. And then I won't ask again. I won't say another word or make any problems for you."

"Make it quick." Shane set her down, and she quickly ducked behind a tree, pressing her back to the trunk, trying to gather herself.

"I don't hear any magic happening. What the fuck are you doing, woman?"

"I can't go when someone's listening," she called out, trying not to shiver. The temperature kept getting colder and colder the closer they got to that mountain.

"I'm not leaving. And you have ten seconds to make it rain or I'm throwing you over my shoulder again."

"Okay! Just…sing for me."

"I'm not going to sing," he scoffed.

"It works every time—you can sing anything. 'Row, Row, Row Your Boat.' 'The Itsy Bitsy Spid—'"

"Eight seconds," he barked.

Shit. Now or never. "I'm going!" She began tiptoeing away, making it several yards before she heard him say she had two seconds left. Liv ran for it, making a sharp right and then another after several seconds, hoping that she and Shane would end up running in opposite directions.

From out of nowhere, Shane caught her arm and practically yanked it from the socket. "Warriors like me have excellent hearing."

"You're hurting me," she growled.

"Consider this being nice. Next time you run, I'll break your leg."

"Nice? You threaten me, bully me, and now you're hurting me."

"The punishment for disobeying your mate is being whipped. The punishment for running from our leader when he's summoned you is losing a foot." He gave her a shake. "Since he sent me to collect you, you've technically done both. So, yes, I'm being nice. Don't run again." Liv heard the anger in his voice. "Do you understand?"

"Yes," she replied, but she wasn't even close to being done. Not until she got the hell off this insane asylum. With Roen.

CHAPTER ELEVEN

Shane scooped Liv into his arms again and continued on through the forest. This theme of getting carted around like a prize goat was getting on her last nerve. That said, she was exhausted and needed the time to think through her next move. Oddly, though, each attempt to initiate any meaningful thoughts was smothered by the odd buzzing coming from Shane's skin. It was the same sensation she'd felt when Roen held her hand. Without anything else to compare it to, the sensation reminded her of a vibrator. Yeah, she had one. What woman didn't these days? All that aside, his touch didn't come anywhere close in the pleasure department.

"Why does your skin do that?" she asked.

"Do what?"

"Buzz."

"You like that?" he asked in a flirty tone.

"No." *God no.* "But you do feel it?"

"Yes. Just like I feel my dick getting hard."

Liv's body tensed.

"Don't worry," he said. "I'm not going to do anything about it." He then added under his breath, "Even though you should be mine."

This was not a conversation she wanted to have, but understanding the threats around her was paramount to her survival. *No time for being optimistic.*

"Because you found me?" she asked.

"The island brought you to *me*. Not Roen."

"I was shipwrecked," she pointed out.

"Who do you think sank your ship?"

"No one," she scoffed. "There was a storm."

"Wrong. The island did it. The island created the storm to bring you here—to me," he added.

"You really believe a hunk of land can do that?"

"I *know* this hunk of land can do that."

"You people are crazy," she mumbled.

"I used to be a psychiatrist. I'd know if I was crazy."

"How's that possible? The psychiatry part, I mean?"

Shane ducked underneath a branch, careful not to get Liv scratched. "I grew up in Kansas City. Went to college. Had a life."

Why would anyone in their right mind come to this place voluntarily? *Roen did. But maybe he's not right in the head either.*

"Why did you leave it?" she asked.

"Same reason as all of the other men. We were conceived here. Eventually, the island calls us back, and we come."

Liv blinked, thinking it over. If what he said was true, then none of the men were from there. It was the same thing Holden had said.

"What does the island want?" she asked, only curious to see what he believed, but not buying one word of the mass delusion.

"Protection from the rest of the world."

Okay. So they were a cult who believed this island was sacred and needed protection.

"Was Roen conceived here, too?" she asked.

"Yes."

Roen had said that he'd come to this island looking for answers. It was plausible that he believed he'd come from this place; however, Roen would have mentioned that.

"What about the women?" she asked.

"What women?" Shane asked.

"Exactly." There weren't any.

He shrugged again, now marching up a steep trail that cut through the forest. He wasn't even winded. "You ask a lot of questions."

You bet your ass I do. How the hell else am I going to figure out how to survive? "That's not an answer."

"The answer is complicated."

"Try me," she shot back.

"Women are not permitted to remain on the island. It's not safe for the—ah. We're here." Shane set her down at the base of a long flight of stone steps lit by torches. At the top looked to be a very big structure, which she couldn't make out. "Roen is waiting for you up there."

"Finish what you were going to say," she demanded.

"Roen is waiting."

In other words, the conversation was over. And now she had a bigger concern, facing Roen.

Liv glanced up toward the top. "I don't think I can make it."

"You'll have to; I'm not permitted to go any further."

Liv would've asked why, but she didn't care. The answer wouldn't help her determine what to do next. On one hand, if Roen was truly up there, she needed to see if he was all right. On the other hand, if he was no longer himself, she'd be putting her life at risk.

"There's nowhere to run, so time to go, sweetheart." Shane gave her a pat on the ass. "Prince Charming awaits."

Liv looked at Shane, wanting so badly to punch him right in his little black skirt. He was right, however, there was nowhere to run. And sadly, she wasn't getting off this island without help. Nor did she want to leave without Roen.

Plus, you'll never rest without knowing if he's dead, alive, or what.

After what felt like the world's longest and most taxing journey, Liv made it to the top of the steps. There was a short, flagstone walkway that led to a hand-carved door. She didn't bother knocking and turned the handle. When the door creaked open, the interior wasn't what she expected. It was a huge modern palace. Smooth white walls displayed fine art—paintings of Poseidon summoning waves with his trident; mermaids perched on a large rock, overlooking the ocean; men, large and nude, emerging from the water and attacking what appeared to be Spanish explorers. Each painting, though beautiful and museum worthy, was also either dark or violent, and a contrast to the bright white walls and abundant recessed lighting. Truly, the home looked like something one might find in a penthouse in New York or the home of an art collector.

"Beautiful, are they not?" said a deep voice.

Liv looked to her right and there, wearing nothing but a piece of suede around his waist, stood Roen with his bulging biceps crossed over his bare chiseled chest.

"Ohmygod. Are you okay?"

Roen dipped his head, but his green eyes held fast to her face and glimmered with a subtle wickedness he hadn't had before. "As you can see."

Yeah, I can see. This Roen seemed to fill the entire room. His arms, which were muscled and large before, looked slightly more menacing. The grooves of his six-pack had deepened. His thighs bulged with power. He was still Roen, but this man now looked more like one of them. Hard. Mean. Dangerous. And yes, just looking at him provoked a primal sexual response.

"What did they do to you?" she asked.

He flashed a sinister grin. "They woke me from the dead."

Liv swallowed. "Roen, how much water did you drink?"

"Come, you must be hungry." He gestured toward the room just opposite of them, across the foyer. "I've had dinner prepared, and there is plenty to drink."

Liv didn't know what to say. He appeared to be in complete control, despite having succumbed to whatever powerful narcotics were in their water. In any case, she wasn't going to let her guard down, just like she wasn't going to ditch the man. Also, running and hiding were no longer options. Survival was now a question of making contact with the outside world, which meant she needed to play this out while proceeding with absolute caution.

Liv looked at Roen and nodded. "I'm starving."

"Right this way, then." Roen led them into a dimly lit, formal dining room big enough to seat at least forty or fifty people. The rectangular, modern-looking, dark wood table stretched from one end of the cavernous room, through a wide doorway, into another room.

"This place is enormous," Liv said, noticing there were three fireplaces—one on each end of the room and one in the center—crackling with logs.

"The style is too pedestrian to suit my tastes, but it will do for now."

His comment reminded her that up until a few days ago, Roen lived in a completely different world where money was no object. They'd never spoken about any of it—when was there time with all the "trying to survive" garbage getting in the way?—but Roen was an industry titan. No doubt his other life was filled with private planes, meetings with important people, extravagant vacations all over the world, and a harem of models or equally gorgeous women.

Immediately, two men, wearing red around their lower torsos, appeared in the room and began setting out dishes filled with steaming food, a bottle of red wine, and a decanter full of ice water. Liv's mouth watered, and Roen must've noticed.

"By all means, help yourself," he said. "And there's no concern about the water. It's from the well—not our sacred water."

Our sacred water. He really had drunk the mer-Kool-Aid, which scared the hell out of her. What if the effects were permanent?

She didn't waste time grabbing the crystal tumbler on the table, filling it up, and gulping down the water. She repeated several times until the water pitcher was almost empty.

Liv wiped her mouth with the back of her hand and glanced over at Roen, who leaned against the wall, large arms folded across his bare, muscular chest, watching her like a hawk. He was eyeing her the same way she had been eyeing that water.

She mentally straightened her spine. It was time to play the game. Only this wasn't a game. "I'm glad you're still alive. I thought something happened to you."

"Never felt better." His gaze was unwavering, penetrating.

"The food smells amazing. Are you going to sit and eat with me?"

His intense green eyes remained stuck to her face. "No. But you go right ahead. You'll need your strength for tonight."

Liv did everything in her power to ignore that comment and not show how terrified it made her feel. She sat down at the place setting near the corner. "You can't just stand there staring while I eat."

Roen gave her a slow nod and sat at the head of the table, just an arm's length away. Yes, he still stared.

She looked down at her empty plate, thinking carefully about her words. She needed to probe the situation so she could assess her possible moves, which included getting Roen home, too. One of the men, with long brown hair tied back into a ponytail, began serving brown rice, followed by steamed vegetables mixed with chunks of white fish. The smell of butter and garlic permeated her nose. She waited for the men to finish serving and leave the room.

"You're really not going to eat?" Liv asked.

"I'm not hungry. And I detest fish." He reached for her glass and filled it with red wine, then his own. "But eat, please."

Liv was starving, but she took only a small bite and chewed carefully. Aside from a few pieces of fruit and some juice, she hadn't eaten in twelve days. *That's your out if he tries anything.* She could very convincingly dissuade him from making any sexual moves if she was hurling on herself. No, it wasn't pleasant, but neither was this situation.

"So," she sipped the wine to help her swallow the food, "I missed you at the beach today."

His sharp gaze continued to threaten her calm façade. "I was busy."

"Oh, I see." She took another small bite.

"There are five thousand years of recorded history, and I must learn it all, including our traditions and secrets, if I am to serve the island well."

He's serious. Ohmygod. He's really serious. "And what did you learn today?"

"That our laws demand you fuck me before the sun rises."

Liv's eyes darted up, and there was no use trying to hide her fear of him any longer. Point being, she felt a very strong attraction for the Roen she just met yesterday, but this wasn't the same person.

He remained still in his chair, leaning back as if they were having a casual conversation about the weather. "I know what you're thinking."

She remained silent while her mind assessed which items on the table could be used as a weapon. *Fork, glass bottle, butter knife…*

"I won't force you, Liv."

"No?" It sure sounded like that.

"Once I explain your options, you'll realize it's what you want. Just like it's what you wanted last night." He leaned in closer. "You want to please the island, too."

Yes, last night a part of her had wanted him. Pretty badly, actually. And yes, the rapid manner in which her insatiable lust for him came on was a little strange. But it was all her, not the island.

She shrugged.

Roen's thick lips curled into a sensual smile. "Ah, you already know what I'm talking about. Don't you, Liv? You heard the island, didn't you?"

No. I'm not crazy. "I had thoughts I couldn't explain, so I'm not sure."

"Then you're lying to yourself. Not that it changes a simple fact: the island gets what the island wants."

"I still have free will," she said flatly. "I'm in control. And so are you."

"Fair enough." He sipped his wine and set down the glass in front of him, the firelight dancing in his eyes. "But when you listen to her, it feels..." He looked up at the ceiling and waved his hand through the air, gesturing while he searched for the words. "It feels like a drug. It feels right."

He spoke as if it truly was a living creature. Very disturbing. "I guess the island and I aren't that close yet."

He tilted his head. "No need to be. That's why there are rules. And approximately two hundred men who will enforce them, which leads me to my point: Everyone must accept their place on this island, and you will be no different."

"What are you going to do to me?"

"I've already done it." He smugly sipped his wine, not breaking eye contact.

Liv's heart pounded in her chest. "What did you do to me?"

"I bit you. And now that you have my mark, the rest is simple. I sleep with you and then we find out what the island has decided."

The conversation made no sense.

"What does it decide?" she asked.

"Whether or not you will carry my child."

She didn't even know how to respond to that other than saying, "That's insane, Roen. Are you listening to yourself talk?"

"Every word."

"I'm not sleeping with you," she said with unwavering conviction.

"If you do not, I will lose my claim on you."

"Uh-uh. I'm not being put up for grabs again." She'd rather die.

He slowly shook his head, a sinister gaze in his green and hazel eyes. "No. You will not be put up for claiming again. I won't allow it."

Now she understood the ugly truth of the ugly conversation: her desire to die instead would be granted. "You'll kill me."

"What will happen is much worse than death."

Liv's eyes involuntarily filled with tears of fear. The only thing worse than death would be torture. *Or being fed alive to those...things.*

"So you see"—he scratched the thick growth of rich brown stubble along his jaw—"why when I say that giving yourself to me—willingly—is your best choice, I speak the truth."

How was that a choice? No, no one had a gun to her head, but what the hell was the difference?

Liv looked away at the flickering fire. *This is crazy. These men are crazy. I'm not doing this.* She looked at Roen and was about to tell him to go stick his "choice" up his unsunny-hole when he winked at her. Yes, a wink. A friendly, playful wink.

Wait. Was he putting on an act? Or was he just being a cocky, brainwashed bastard? Liv felt a tiny burst of relief. She wanted to believe he could never hurt her.

Roen pushed away from the long table and adjusted the suede around his waist. He looked less savage than the other men with his short hair and tattoo-free body, but he carried himself with every ounce of caged ferocity as the rest of them.

"After you're done eating," Roen said, "my men will show you to your room upstairs. You will bathe, dress, and do as they say."

Not in a million years. She bobbed her head yes.

"Enjoy your meal."

"Where are you going?" she asked so she could gauge how much time she had to run like hell. *Or stay. If he's putting on an act, then he doesn't mean a word he just said.*

His eyes narrowed on her face, and his skin flushed. He was angry. Enraged even. "I think you're forgetting your place, woman. Now eat and do what I've asked before I get angry."

He left the room with wide heavy strides while Liv's mouth gaped open.

What the hell is going on? Clearly, there were eyes and ears all over the goddamned place, so it would make absolute sense that he wouldn't jeopardize their chances of escaping by breaking character. On the other hand, Roen had told her that he was infected. He'd felt himself losing control.

Take a breath, Liv, and weigh your options. She was out in the middle of the goddamned ocean on an island no one knew existed. She had no means of escape without Roen. Running and hiding wasn't a long-term option either. Not only was the island far too small, but these men seemed to have the hunting instincts of wolves.

Okay, sharks.

In any case, roaming around in that forest at night was not a smart move either. Whatever those…those things were on the beach, they scared the crap out of her.

So that leaves you one choice: roll the dice with Roen, and hope he's still in control. If he showed any signs of having completely lost it, she would be ready to knock him hard with a vase or chair or… She looked around the room. *Some really, really strange art?*

She quickly gulped down her wine and finished her rice. Minutes later, the same two men appeared and removed her empty plate. *The red-skirts were watching you.* They'd probably been listening to her entire conversation with Roen, too.

"Thank you," she said. "By the way, why do some of you wear red?"

The one with sandy blond hair shot her a look.

"Sorry. Didn't mean to offend your merman senses," she said.

"Your question isn't offensive. But a landlover female should know her place."

What he really meant to say was that *she* was offensive and had no right asking questions.

"I know my place—it's called home—and I'm more than happy to go there. Care to help me?"

They ignored her snide comment and showed her upstairs to a spacious room with bright white carpets and walls and more dramatic sea creature art of intertwining eels. There was an inviting king-sized bed—God, how she missed beds—covered in soft white linens and a large bathroom tiled in natural stone with a large sunken tub and walk-in shower. The room was pristine, modern, and impersonal and a complete contradiction to the uncivilized men on the island.

As soon as they left, Liv turned on the shower and began searching the room for a weapon, but there was little there aside from a black dress—a knit T-shirty thing—and some towels. Even the hangers in the closet were plastic, not wire.*Plastic. On an island like this*. It was utterly surreal.

If Roen got out of hand, she would have to make do with the bulbous stainless steel lamps on the nightstands.

She jumped into the shower, quickly washing away the sticky mud on her arms and the sweat from her body. Until she knew for sure where Roen's head was at, she needed to play along.

Dammit. I can't get the smell out. Bits of dried shark blood had remained stuck in her hair, and she wondered if she'd ever feel clean again after these past few days. Of course, these men didn't seem to care. They looked like they bathed every other full moon. Surprisingly, however, they didn't stink—well, not in a bad way. Most of them smelled like a concoction of fresh sweat, cinnamon, and earth. Not offensive.

She finished scrubbing as quickly as possible, trying to ignore her pounding head from lack of sleep.

She emerged from the shower and wrapped a white towel around her body. When she opened the bathroom door, a large, shirtless male figure sat on the bed. She yelped from instinct, but it was Roen, his hard muscular frame propped against the hand-carved headboard.

"You scared the hell out of me," she said.

He didn't respond to that, instead staring with those deep green eyes with inner rings of hazel. "Come closer."

She didn't move. Not until she knew what she was dealing with.

"Did you not hear me?"

"I heard you," she replied.

"Then why are you still standing there?"

She shrugged. If he was still trying to help her and his men were listening, she couldn't ask him point blank if he was playing a charade. Then again, if he were faking, why couldn't he wink again or make a gesture to indicate his true intention?

Before she uttered another word, he sprang from the bed, grabbed her wrist and threw her down on the bed. He quickly covered her mouth with his hand. "Be quiet and listen," he whispered, "the island is watching. She knows everything—sees everything."

Ohmygod. Roen actually believed they were being watched by the fucking island.

He began kissing her neck, his free hand roaming over her breasts. Liv didn't know what to do.

His lips once again journeyed back to her ear. "Just before dawn, go through the kitchen, out the back door and head to the beach east of the island. It's one mile from here. The crew of my ship will not be able to see the island, so you have to swim out at least one hundred yards. But whatever you do, do not get into the water before the sun rises. Do you understand?"

His soft lips moved back to her neck and massaged her breast, grinding himself against her.

He *was* putting on an act. An act for the island. How crazy was that?

She nodded, and he removed his hand from her mouth.

"Don't ever come back here," he whispered. "Not for me, not for anything."

Liv jerked her head back and their eyes met. He had absolutely no intention of leaving. *No, he has to come. He has to.*

She mouthed the word "please," and Roen knew exactly what she meant but shook his head.

Liv's heart filled with a new fear: Roen might be punished or killed once the men found out he'd let her go.

He's not stupid, Liv. He's got to be thinking about covering his tracks somehow.

God, she hoped so, but any way the situation played out, this place would eat him alive. The worst part was she'd never see him again and she genuinely wanted to. She'd never met anyone like Roen; so goddamned crazy and damaged and fearless. On the outside, he seemed like this cold, uncaring person who only cared about money, but people like that didn't take risks for strangers like he'd done. *Like he's doing now.*

"Roen, I don't want you to stay here. It's starting to change you, and I really, really like you just the way you are."

Roen stared back with an intense gaze, somewhere between joy and sadness, but nowhere close to content.

"Please, I'm begging you," she whispered. "Because I don't think I can leave here witho—"

He cut her off with a kiss.

Without you, she wanted to say. But his full, silky lips and the sensual stroke of his tongue completely melted her from head to toe, triggering that voice—the one that told her to let him slip off her towel. The one that told her she really did want to have sex with him.

Sensual aches swept through her body, effortlessly untying those knots of apprehension as they charged their way between her legs. The weight of his strong, hard body on top of her, the heated touch of his hand, and those determined lips surrounded by bristly stubble left Liv paralyzed by her need for him.

"I want you," he growled in a low husky voice. "I can't stop thinking about you." Roen reached for the front of her towel and kissed his way down to her chest, peeling back the white terry cloth, exposing her chest.

A moment of self-consciousness flickered inside her head. She knew the last few weeks had thinned her normally curvy body, but Roen's deep throaty groan as he looked at her bare breasts relieved any timidness.

His mouth slid over her right nipple, sucking and kissing, while his other hand massaged the left. She'd never felt anything so delicious, like that buzzy energy amplified the pleasure of his touch. She began to see why women would give themselves voluntarily—a strange, strange thought. But not as strange as how empty her body felt and how badly she craved the sexual pleasure he could deliver with that thick cock between his legs.

Roen's hand slid down her torso and between her thighs. The moment his thick warm fingers slid between her soft folds, gliding over her throbbing bud, she let out a soft moan. Roen began kissing his way down her stomach while his fingers found their way inside her, pushing gently at first, not so gently after a few seconds. When his mouth and heated tongue joined with the deep penetration of his fingers, Liv writhed on the bed, her hips pressing harder into him. What the hell was he doing? It felt so damned good.

His tongue worked at a relentless pace, sliding and kneading with exquisite pressure as that warm hand pumped. She felt her body slipping further and further away from reality and from the situation, leaving only her and Roen, there on that bed, their bodies' rhythms the only thing that mattered. In that moment, if he wanted to fuck her, her only objection would have been him stopping what he was doing with his mouth.

She glanced down at Roen, whose eyes were closed, seemingly lost in the act of pleasuring her with his mouth. She was about to pull him up, to tell him she wanted him inside her, but she watched his free hand slide down to grip his erection. His size, from the glimpse she'd seen, was pure magnificence—thick and long and so hard that it could've been cut from marble.

She'd never watched anything more erotic, and in that moment, she felt her nerve endings wind up and burst open, shooting waves of hard contractions pulsing through her core. A moan escaped her mouth as she grabbed fistfuls of sheets and arched her entire body toward his vigorously sucking mouth.

After a moment, she looked back down at Roen, whose green eyes had been watching her come with intense pleasure. He crawled his way up her body, still pumping his long thick cock with his large hand at a leisurely pace as if enjoying every second. When he laid his body over her again, she was sure he planned to push his way inside and make her come all over again, but instead he kissed her hard, the taste of herself all over his mouth. His hand stayed between them, pumping his cock for several moments and then he broke away and pushed up with one arm. He looked down at himself as he exploded, shooting his cum onto her stomach. Liv had never watched a man come, and she'd certainly never imagined she'd find it so sinfully erotic.

Eyes closed, Roen stilled for a moment, releasing those final drops, and then lay to her side to catch his breath. Meanwhile Liv's head spun in delicious, post-orgasmic circles, urging her to sleep.

No. Don't sleep. You have to do something to convince him to leave with you.

Roen abruptly stood from the bed and went to the bathroom, returning with a warm, damp washcloth. He wiped her clean and threw it into a basket in the corner before laying down beside her again. She still hadn't really moved, perhaps because she was too in shock, perhaps because her body was still floating around somewhere high up in the clouds.

Roen didn't touch or kiss her. Instead he lay naked on his back, staring at the ceiling, an intense expression on his face.

"Why didn't you…" Her voice trailed off. It was a stupid question. Obviously, neither of them carried any birth control. In fact, what had she been thinking? Because she would've let him. No question about it. *This place is messing with my head.* That didn't mean the pull to be with him wasn't real; it simply meant that being reckless wasn't her style.

"Have sex with you?" he said.

"Yeah."

"You didn't ask me to." She hadn't asked him to do anything he'd just done, but he'd done it anyway. And it was incredible. "It's the law. The woman must ask to be fucked."

"Oh." She was about to say she'd remember that next time, when they were hopefully armed with a box of condoms, but there wouldn't be a next time. *Not if you don't convince him to leave.*

"That and I care about you too much," he added.

Her heart fell down a deep dark hole. He could've told her about the "law" but hadn't. Likely to protect her from making this mess any bigger than it already was.

"Roen?"

His eyes glanced at her for a moment but quickly returned to staring at the ceiling.

She wanted to beg him to come with her, but she already knew he wasn't going to leave. Was it really because of his brother, or was there another reason?

"Is your brother all right?" she asked.

"Yes. He's happy here. It's his home."

"So he never wants to leave."

"No," he replied.

Then staying to help Lyle wasn't the reason. "And you?" She hoped his answer might be different.

"No."

She hadn't expected him to tip his hand at any plans for escape, but there was no doubt in his voice. It sounded like he wanted to shut the door on her having any hope.

"I don't believe you," she said.

"You don't have to. It won't change a thing."

"I don't think you understand how much—"

"Don't." He looked at her like he wanted to say something but caught himself. "The sun will be up soon, and I have a long day ahead." He shut off the lamp on the nightstand and coldly turned his back to her. He was trying to tell her to leave now. He'd said that she needed to run out the back and head to the beach before it got light out.

Liv lay there for much longer than she should've, resisting the urge to stay and "ask" him, to spend just ten more minutes with him.

Roen's hand slid over hers and gave it a comforting squeeze. The gesture nearly broke her.

Dammit, Liv. If you care anything about him, you'll get the hell off this island and bring back help. Even if it required force because he was too delusional to help himself. It was the only way.

"Good night, Roen. You'll be in my dreams."

She heard a faint chuckle—as if the thought pleased him. Within a few minutes, Roen's breathing turned steady and rhythmic. This was it. She slipped from the bed and grabbed the black dress hanging in the closet, slipping it quickly over her head as she tiptoed from the room.

With every step she took, the cells in her body protested more violently, screaming at her not to do this. *But you'll be back for him. You'll see him again*, she told herself. Then why did she feel the bond between them ripping away? *There's no other choice. If you stay here, you'll die.* Or worse, as Roen had told her. *And if you stay, who will send help for him?* The moment she stepped foot on his ship and alerted his crew, she had to believe the entire world would descend upon this godforsaken place looking for him. A man like Roen—powerful and wealthy—was the type of man people would expend considerable resources on to rescue.

As silently as possible, she followed the stairs back down to the dining room and into the kitchen. The entire house was dark and quiet, but Roen's men couldn't be far.

With only a bit of moonlight shining through a window over a bank of stainless steel sinks, she felt her way through the kitchen until she reached the back door. Liv carefully pulled it open and slipped outside.

Just a few yards from the house, Liv found a narrow trail leading down the hill. Bright white rocks lining each side of the narrow path reflected the bit of moonlight, guiding the way. Once far enough away, she began a fast walk, hoping to God she didn't come across any of those damned monsters. Or another sharp rock. *Ouch!* Without shoes, every little twig and stone seemed intent on finding their way between her toes.

I don't need my toes, I just need to live. For her family, for Roen, for herself.

After about thirty minutes, the familiar sound of crashing waves roared in the distance. She was close, but Roen had said not to get into the water before the sun came up. Not that she intended to. But it wouldn't be long now. The sky had already turned from a dark gray to a deep lavender.

"Where the fuck do you think you're going, landlover?" said a deep voice.

Liv turned and saw a man with darkish hair down to his waist, covered head-to-toe in tribal tattoos, leaning against a tall pine tree just a few feet away. She didn't recognize him, but that didn't matter. The look on his face set off every female alarm bell in her body.

"Guess Roen didn't get lucky last night, which sounds like a forfeit on his claim. Must be my lucky day instead." His eyes flashed to her now completely healed shoulder, which showed no signs of Roen's bite mark.

Then, from the corner of Liv's eye, she spotted a set of lights off in the distance, moving back and forth over the water. *Searchlights! It's the ship.* But the sun still wasn't up, and God only knew what would happen if she got into the water.

The man reached for her arm and lowered his mouth, flashing his white teeth, intent on sinking them into her.

Hell no! Liv jerked away and ran as fast as she could toward the ocean. Whatever was in it might deter him from coming after her and the sun would be out in a matter of minutes. *You can make it. You can make it, Liv.* Arms pumping and legs thrusting,

Liv ran for her life. Ten feet from the water's edge her body tumbled into the sand. The bastard had tripped her from behind.

He flipped her over, and Liv screamed, "Get the hell off me!"

The man's hard features became visible as the sky became lighter. He had a thick scar across his right cheek and a ruthless look in his eyes. "That's right, landlover, fight. The island said you would. She also said I could break the laws if I caught you."

Liv assumed he meant the worst and twisted and kicked with everything she had. However, her malnourished body was no match for this colossal beast. He moved to straddle her, pinning her hands above his head. With a sinister gleam in his eyes, he slowly moved his head toward her neck.

Fuck! He was going to bite her. These men were lunatics.

"Nooo!" She released a bloodcurdling yell and felt his teeth sinking into her skin. Suddenly, her face was covered in warm wet liquid. Liv thought it was her own blood, but the man began screaming in agony, falling to her side. Blood was everywhere—in her mouth, in her eyes, covering her face.

Then she saw them: five black forms descending on the man like hungry wolves.

That blood's not mine. Liv blinked, her mind trying to make out the shapes of the animals. But the way they moved and slithered together over the man as he screamed, his limbs flailing and punching, made them difficult to see.

Suddenly, the sun broke over the horizon and a few small rays of light washed over the water and beach. The animals howled and hissed, quickly retreating into the water.

All but one.

No longer feeding, the monster came into focus, its wide yellow eyes glowing against charcoal black skin.

Ohmyfuckinggod. Liv wanted to run, but she couldn't. *It can't be. It can't fucking be...*

It wasn't just a monster; it was a woman. A woman who looked like she was coated in thick tar, whose hair hung in ropes of drippy black seaweed. But she wasn't exactly a woman either. The thing had humanlike features, including breasts, until halfway down its body. From the navel down, however, its skin was scaly like a fish. Instead of legs, it had a long tail that bent back like she had knees somewhere underneath that horror-show costume.

Liv screamed at the top of her lungs, and the thing raised its index finger to its bloody mouth. "Sssshhh," it hissed. The sun brightened across the thing's face, but unlike the others, it didn't seem affected.

"Wha-what do you want?" Liv whispered.

"I have a message from the island." The woman's voice was raspy and low. "You may leave, but you must promise never to tell. Not about the island. Not about any of us. If you do, our men will come for you. They will know, and they will come for you. Do you understand?"

Liv nodded without even realizing it.

The creature smiled, displaying a set of razor-sharp pearly whites, and then reached down, snatching something from around the dead man's neck. She chucked it at Liv. "Drink it. It will stop the bleeding on your neck."

Liv's hand moved to the spot where the man had bitten her. She didn't feel any pain—too scared out of her mind for that.

The beast reached for the man's limp arm and began tugging him toward the ocean.

Holy shit. She's taking her kill with her.

"Wait," Liv said. "Are you what happens to the women who come here?"

The thing just looked at her with a pained expression. "Sometimes." Then it slowly turned and pulled the bloody body with her, disappearing into the waves.

It took several moments for Liv to believe what she'd actually just witnessed. It was all too surreal—the horror of watching a man torn apart by goddamned mermaids. But not mermaids at all—not like the ones in fairytales, anyway.

Ohmygod. The boat! Liv got to her feet and spotted the ship off in the distance, perhaps even a bit closer now. Yes, she could make it, but those things were in the water.

If they were going to hurt you, they would've. Go!

She stepped into the waves, but something tugged inside her mind. *Wait. If I leave, then what about Roen?* That thing had told her she couldn't ever tell anyone about the island.

I have to go back for him. Liv turned and froze. Just outside the tree line stood Roen with a tormented look in his green eyes. *Why's he standing there?*

"Roen! Look!" She pointed toward the ship.

He didn't move toward her. Instead, he lifted his hand to wave goodbye.

"Roen! Goddammit," she yelled. "Please!"

Roen looked at his bare feet and turned away, heading into the forest.

Oh God. He's really staying. But what possible motive could he have? She couldn't think of one goddamned reason. He'd already told her that his brother was happy, so it wasn't like the man needed to be rescued. Then there was the fact that Roen had a life, a pretty damned big one, back in the real world. Something was keeping him here, but what?

She took a deep breath, feeling a pull so strong, it nearly ripped her in two. She wanted to go after him, to make him come with her.

Liv glanced over her shoulder at the boat. *Dammit.* She'd never survive if she stayed. *Think about your family. Think about Dana and Krista.* Was going after Roen worth the rest of her life with the people she loved? Was it worth risking her life?

She looked down at the salt water swishing around her knees.

Suddenly, Liv was running as fast as she could toward the shore, but as she reached the beach, the sand beneath her dissolved into nothing. She felt her body falling forward, but when she thrust out her hands to break her fall, there was nothing but water.

Heart pounding, she managed to bring her head out of the water and gasp for air, but when she looked up, the island was gone.

"Look! Over there!" a man's voice yelled off in the distance. Then the sound of a loud siren filled her ears.

"No, no, no!" *Where the fuck is the island?* Treading water, Liv spun in a circle, searching for any sign of the damned thing, but there was nothing except miles of open water and that enormous cargo ship.

She suddenly heard a loud splash and the sound of a small motor. She looked over her shoulder as a military-style raft approached with two men aboard.

No, goddammit! Sobbing, she started swimming back toward the direction of where the island had to be, but the current pushed her back. When the men finally reached her, she felt like her soul had been ripped in two. She was saved, but she'd left something important on that island: a piece of her heart.

☙❧

Roen walked away from Liv and let out a slow breath. Getting her off the island had not been as easy as he'd thought, but it was done, and that was all that mattered. It didn't mean, however, he wouldn't regret it for the rest of his life or regret the deal he'd just had to strike with the island to make it all happen.

"Brother." Lyle stood on the path, arms folded over his chest. "I heard the news about your mate."

"Who told you?" Roen asked.

Lyle raised a dark brow as if to say, "Who do you think?"

Roen simply nodded. Of course. The island had. Which meant Lyle also knew what Liv's freedom had just cost him and would cost others. "Yeah, well."

"The island cannot read your mind, but once you've let her in, she can read what's in your heart. You can't ever deceive her."

Roen knew that now. While he'd been with Liv, he'd tried to block out his torment over knowing he'd never see her again. But that had been impossible. The island knew all along what he'd intended to do. Simply put, it was a miracle she'd not been killed.

It was also a miracle he'd resisted Liv the way he had when every cell in his body cried out for her. He'd wanted to fuck her five different ways until sunrise and then spend the entire day making it up to her with long baths and slow lovemaking. But had he done that, Liv's life as she knew it would've been over, and he simply couldn't do that to the only woman he'd ever felt anything for. Yes, he'd done one decent and right thing in his life by saving Liv.

I just hope that's enough to carry you through what will come next.

"You must let her go." Lyle reached out and squeezed Roen's shoulder.

Roen nodded. "I already have."

"Good. Because you managed to do the one thing I could not."

Roen looked at Lyle, waiting for the answer.

"To save someone they cared about from ending up on this island."

CHAPTER TWELVE

Two Months Later.

This was a mistake. She'll lock me up if I tell the truth. Cold sweaty hands fisted tightly, Liv shifted on the brown leather armchair and stared out the window overlooking the empty courtyard of the small office complex. As usual for this time of year in Wrangell, Alaska, it was cool but sunny outside, and just the sort of late spring day that used to get her into the garden.

Not anymore. Now she hated being outdoors.

"Ms. Stratton?" Dr. June, a woman in her late sixties, sat patiently across from Liv.

"Liv. Call me Liv," she muttered, avoiding full eye contact.

Dr. June uncrossed her legs and set her notepad on the doily-covered glass coffee table between them. "All right, Liv. You came to see me because you wanted help, but you haven't spoken once in three sessions, so why don't you try to tell me what's on your mind? I'm not going to judge; I promise."

"I can't," Liv whispered. "I thought I could, but I can't." The memories were just too painful, and she didn't know how to organize the chaos inside her head in a way that would make sense to her, let alone a psychiatrist. But she knew she needed this. So very badly.

"It's very common to feel that way, Liv. You survived a traumatic event. But I always tell my patients to start with something easy and small. Just see where it goes."

That was the problem; she'd survived. And what had started out as a very publicized but emotional, joyous reunion with her family, who'd believed she'd died, had turned into a nightmare.

The media had gotten wind that she'd been found in the middle of the North Pacific by one of Roen Doran's cargo ships after they'd received a mysterious call from him instructing them to come back for her. Obviously, the world wondered where the hell he was, because the last thing anyone knew for certain was that his helicopter had gone down near where they'd rescued Liv. In addition, five of Roen's crew had taken one of the small boats from the ship, looking for survivors after his chopper went down. They never returned.

Of course, Liv knew why, and everyone looked to her for all the answers, especially the part about Roen. First the Coast Guard and FBI, then Roen's lawyer—some guy named Phil, who told her he'd ruin her "pathetic white-trash existence" if she didn't tell him what she knew regarding Roen's whereabouts. Where the hell did anyone get off saying that kind of garbage to another person? Her father was an insurance broker and her mother worked as a bookkeeper. They weren't filthy rich like Roen, but that Phil sleazeball spoke to her like she was nothing because of it. She hung up on the a-hole, and then things got really bad. Was he behind it? She didn't know, but the tabloids printed made-up stories about her being involved in some kidnapping plot. The news channels and papers joined in and showed pictures of her, even naming her hometown. For Christ's sake, Wrangell's population was only two thousand four hundred. They might as well have given out her home address to the entire world.

"I don't know anything," she'd told them all. "The fishing boat went down. I was in a raft for twelve days, and it finally deflated. A ship rescued me just in time, but I never saw or spoke to anyone." And when they asked her to explain Roen's call to his ship, she simply said she couldn't. Luckily, the authorities didn't believe any of the horrific accusations, but that didn't mean they believed her lies either. Even her parents called her out, telling her if she knew something, it was her obligation to say so. But none of that gigantic cluster compared to her guilt over Roen. He was still on that island. And no one would be coming to help him. No one.

"Liv?" Dr. June leaned closer. "Liv, honey, there's nothing to be afraid of. You're safe now, and no one can hurt you here."

Was that really true? Because Liv's frantically beating heart told her she was anything but safe.

"I'm—I'm not sure coming here was a good idea," Liv said, tugging at the collar of her red turtleneck.

"Of course it was. Just take a moment to gather your thoughts. You're my last appointment of the day, so I'll wait as long as you need."

That could be a hell of a long time.

"May I?" Liv glanced at the water cooler in the corner next to the bookshelf full of cat memorabilia and snow globes. She thanked her lucky stars that the psychiatrist wasn't into fish. Liv didn't want to think about anything with fins.

"Of course, dear. Help yourself." Dr. June flashed a comforting smile.

Liv got up and crossed the homey, knickknack-filled office, refusing to look at herself in the beveled mirror stuck to the wall for those "get in touch with yourself" sessions. Seeing her reflection—bloodshot brown eyes and unkempt brown hair—only reminded her of the mess she'd become.

Liv took a paper cup from the dispenser and filled it up. Suddenly, words bubbled from her mouth. "They said that they'd come for me if I told anyone. That they would know." Liv closed her eyes for a moment, waiting for the sky to fall. Of course, it didn't.

Okay. See. That wasn't so hard and nothing bad happened.

"Keep going, Liv. Who told you they'd come for you?"

Liv gulped down her water, but kept her back to Dr. June. *Don't be afraid. Don't be afraid. You can do this.*

She ran one hand over the back of her head. "The problem is, they weren't…" She wanted to say they weren't human. And after she'd seen those creatures on the beach, she now knew that everything she'd heard on that island was true. So perhaps it was true that they'd hunt her down and kill her if she broke her promise to stay silent. If they did, what would happen to her family? They'd just gotten her back. But Liv simply couldn't stop the nightmares. She couldn't let go of what she'd seen and what she'd done. Worst of all, she couldn't let go of Roen. Every thought led back to him.

How could I have left him behind? He saved me, and I left him with those savages. It didn't matter that he'd stayed of his own free will. The man hadn't been well. But she'd left him with no hope of rescue. Why? Because she'd promised never to tell anyone about the island. She should've said no, but Liv had been terrified for her life. Especially after she learned what those men did to women. It was unspeakable.

"Liv, here's what I'd like you to do." Dr. June stood and handed Liv her notepad and pen. "I want you to write down what you can't say. Then I'll read it and we'll burn it together in the trash can.

That way, no one but us will ever know what you wrote. Okay?"

Liv nodded her head. She had to tell someone. She needed to figure out what to do.

Liv took the pen and paper, but couldn't make her hand move. *You're being irrational. You need to tell her. You need help.* Liv hadn't slept in two months and could barely eat. She'd been unable to return to her life in Seattle, where she attended school, or function in any normal way. She was spiraling hard.

Liv scribbled one word on the paper and handed it to Dr. June.

Dr. June read it and frowned with a deeply disturbed expression. "I don't understand. You think mermen are coming to get you?"

Yes, and part of me wants them to. I deserve to be punished.

Liv replied yes and in that moment, a powerful wave of painful pinpricks exploded. Her body began to convulse uncontrollably, and she tumbled to the floor.

"Liv!" The doctor jumped from her seat and called for help. "Liv! Can you hear me?" But all Liv could do was clench her teeth as the excruciating pain barreled through her veins like molten lava pushing its way through her skin, trying to break free. Suddenly, it did. The pain evaporated, and she could almost taste it in the air, rising above her body.

The doctor told her assistant to call nine-one-one then turned her attention back to Liv. "Try to breathe, Liv. Just try to breathe. An ambulance will be here in a few minutes," Dr. June said.

Liv gasped and held her trembling hand over her mouth. She knew. She somehow knew what had just happened. *It was a beacon.*

"Oh my God," she whispered. *They know. And now they're coming for me.*

"Liv, just try to breathe slowly."

Liv heard the sirens off in the distance and sat up. An ambulance wasn't going to help her. Nothing could.

"No. You lie still." The doctor gently pushed back on her shoulder, but Liv didn't want to be put in the position of being asked anymore questions.

"I'm fine. I think it was just a panic attack or something."

"Liv, you looked like you were having a seizure."

Liv got to her feet. "I'm fine. I promise."

"I can't let you leave here like this." The doctor crossed her arms. "You said you saw mermen. You said you think they're coming for you."

Liv laughed. "I didn't mean literally. I've been having these nightmares. That's all. I'm really, really tired."

The doctor stared at her. "I'm not letting you get behind the wheel of a car. I'd be a poor doctor if I did."

Two female paramedics burst into the room. Of course, they didn't see anyone who appeared injured or sick, so that made them pause.

"Liv, let them check you out."

"Or?"

"Or I'll tell them to put you under psychiatric evaluation."

Liv wanted to strangle the damned woman, but what choice did she have now? "Fine. I'll go with them."

Dr. June smiled. "Very good, Liv." She turned her head toward the paramedics. "My patient seems to have experienced a seizure. Please be sure they look her over thoroughly."

After five hours of blood work, a CT scan, and heart monitoring, the ER doctor—an African American woman about the same age as Liv, with a petite frame and short dark hair—came by to check on her. Liv was doing her best to stay calm so she'd be released quickly, but it felt like a giant target had been painted on her back and the clock was ticking.

Where would she go? Would they come after her family, too? Perhaps she should get out of town, but that wasn't easy given how far Wrangell was from just about anything. One hundred and five miles to Ketchikan and about two hundred to Juneau or Naukati Bay. Of course, those routes were by plane or boat because driving to or from Wrangell was impossible.

Another goddamned island.

Liv gave it some thought and decided it was better to risk bumping into press at the local inn than jeopardizing her family. In the morning, she'd figure something out.

"So...Liv. I'm Dr. Fuller." The woman flipped through the charts. "Everything's come back normal—no signs of hemorrhages or tumors. And the nurse said you haven't experienced any head trauma."

Sitting up on the bed, Liv rubbed her hands over her face. "I'm fine. Just tired, that's all. Not getting a lot of sleep since…you know." It wasn't like there were any secrets in this town.

"I can give you something to help you sleep, but please make an appointment with your regular physician next week for a follow-up."

Liv nodded. "Thanks. I'll do that."

"That's odd." The doctor's eyes stuck on the final page of whatever lab reports she was looking at. "You've got some…" The woman paused and scratched her cheek before looking at Liv. "Ms. Stratton, have you taken any illegal substances?"

"What? No. I don't do drugs."

"The pathologist commented that there's an unknown compound in your blood."

"Like what?" Liv asked.

"You're sure you haven't taken anything, been exposed to any chemicals?"

Liv shook her head. "No. Nothing."

"It's probably a lab error. Happens sometimes."

Liv shrugged, trying not to draw suspicion.

"All right, Liv. See the nurse on the way out for your prescription. If you start to feel worse, don't hesitate to come back."

Liv got up from the bed and put on her jeans, red sweater, and boots. Her head tingled, and she felt a mild burning sensation in her veins. The doctor's comments about finding something in her blood hadn't shocked her one bit. She *knew* something was inside her—that damned water—and it scared the hell out of her.

It was almost eleven o'clock when Liv left the ER, planning to walk to the inn over on the waterfront, but the moment she exited the building, an extremely tall, very muscular man in a black suit, standing next to a black SUV with tinted windows, stopped her in her tracks.

Oh shit.

"Hello, Ms. Stratton," he said and dipped his head of long, dreaded black hair.

Liv didn't reply. Should she run? Should she go back inside and ask for help? *They can't help you and running won't do any good.*

"That was fast," she finally said.

The man, who she knew for sure was one of them but didn't recognize, opened the passenger door. "Get in."

Liv's boots stuck to the ground.

"Don't make this any worse than it needs to be," he warned.

Liv nodded solemnly and slid into the backseat. Once the man was behind the wheel, starting the engine, she asked where they were going, but he wouldn't answer.

"Okay. Then you might as well kill me now because I won't go all the way back to that island just so you can do it there."

The driver flashed a quick glance at her through the rearview mirror. Even in the dark, those green eyes were unsettling. "I am not taking you to the island. Roen is in Seattle, attending to business."

Roen was off the island? *Ohmygod. Ohmygod.* The relief was immeasurable. Liv placed a fisted hand over her heart. *Thank. God.* But why hadn't he contacted her?

Doesn't matter. If he was all right and safe and...alive, then everything she'd suffered through was worth it.

CHAPTER THIRTEEN

It was two in the morning when Liv arrived at the skyscraper apartment building in downtown Seattle. The flight on Roen's private plane had felt too surreal for words, partially because it was difficult imagining the man she knew living this other life— luxury, wealth, power. More difficult to reconcile, however, was that Roen had made it off the island but was still involved with these men. It didn't make sense.

When her "escort"—the man who'd picked her up at the hospital—opened the limo door, Liv couldn't contain her happiness. Seeing Roen again was the only thing she'd thought of for eight weeks. It had carried her through the unbearable chaos that had become her life.

The man walked Liv into the brightly lit lobby with gleaming black marble floors and a glass pane sculpture in the middle. Water sheeted silently over both sides of the glass, reflecting the lights above, making the space feel like one of those viewing rooms at an aquarium.

After signing them in, the security guard directed her and the escort toward the stainless steel elevator doors to the penthouse. As the elevator rose to the thirtieth floor, Liv felt her hands and knees shake with anticipation. What would she say to him? Would she tell him that not a second went by these last few months when she wasn't thinking about him or regretting her decision to leave him? Would she tell him that resisting the pull to go back to him felt like having her body torn in two, piece by piece, cell by cell? No, he'd think she was crazy. They barely knew each other.

Don't say that. Loving someone isn't crazy. Liv stepped from the elevator and froze. *Oh crap. I love him.* She knew she cared and felt an insanely strong attraction, but the love thing had snuck up on her. She'd never loved a man. Not like this.

The driver hung back and watched her approach the door. "He's expecting you. Go in," the man said.

She reached for the handle and then paused. What if this was a trap? What if she didn't find Roen behind that door, but another one of those cruel men—

The door flew open and there stood Roen in an elegant, charcoal gray suit. His skin looked darker, like he spent his days outside, and his hair had grown out quite a bit, reaching his jawline, giving him a slightly more rugged look. It too seemed darker than before, more of a rich brown versus his caramel brown. Liv's eyes ran up and down his sleek, muscular frame, taking him in. Roen appeared to be a few inches bigger in each direction—taller, broader shoulders, and slightly more muscular, but still not as large as those tanks who called themselves mermen.

Despite the shocking changes, Liv had never seen a more beautiful man. Not even Roen's airbrushed cover photo for Sexiest Man of the Year had looked as stunning as he did now.

Roen stared down at her with cold eyes, those slightly full lips in a straight line, framed by a thick covering of facial hair, the length somewhere between a beard and overgrown stubble.

"Ms. Stratton, it's nice to see you." His voice was barren of any real welcoming, immediately setting the tone. He stepped aside and gestured for her to enter, but she hesitated. His tensing jaw and rigid posture, almost like a soldier in formation, told her he was holding his rage at bay.

Liv instinctually stepped back.

Roen continued staring with those icy, displeased eyes. "There's nowhere you can hide. Not from me. Not from them."

"So you're going to hurt me."

"You broke a promise to the island, Liv. I'm the only thing standing between you and hurt. So I suggest you come inside."

She hesitantly moved past him, and he closed the door behind her. The penthouse had an open floorplan—living room, kitchen, dining room in one space—with simple yet sophisticated furniture, mostly brown and black colors with white walls.

"Why don't you take a seat?" He gestured toward a set of light gray sofas that faced each other over a glass coffee table. A low flame flickered away in the gas fireplace just to the side of the table.

"Thank you." She sat at the end of one couch closest to the fireplace and focused on her breathing—a better option than her trembling hands or pounding heart.

Roen walked to the kitchen area—with glass cabinets, stainless steel everything, and a large granite island in the middle. He poured two glasses of red wine and walked over to the sitting area, handing one to her.

"Here. You'll need this," he said.

She stared up at Roen's imposing frame, trying not to acknowledge the conflicting feelings he brought out in her. Half of her heart buzzed with joy at the sight of him. The other half felt terrified.

He won't hurt you, Liv. Just stay calm. That's what she told herself, anyway. Truth was, she had no clue what he planned to do with her.

"So." She cleared her throat. "How did you get off of the island?"

Roen slid off his blazer and folded it neatly over the arm of the sofa opposite her before taking a seat.

"Turns out…" He began rolling up his sleeves, exposing his thick forearms. Yes, he'd definitely grown, but was still lean and predator-like. Not a rhino like the other men. "Turns out there are about fifty or so large yachts on the island. Along with a small plane and a landing strip."

"Why didn't we see them?"

"The island didn't wish us to see them." He finished rolling up his sleeve and leaned back.

"So it just let you leave?"

"I'm not a prisoner, Liv. I lead the island because I want to."

Liv didn't believe that.

"Once you left and I was free of distraction," he continued, "Lyle was able to help me truly come to understand my purpose—what I must do."

She stared expectantly.

"The island requires assistance," he elaborated, "and I plan to give it."

"Assistance." She repeated the word, hoping she'd misheard him.

"She won't stay hidden from the world forever, and the island needs better defenses, which means modern equipment and people with training."

Liv shifted on the couch, trying to process what Roen said without automatically jumping to any conclusions. Because despite the impossibility of it all, Liv had seen and felt things that proved there was much more to that island than dirt and rock.

"Okay," she said. "But what about your company and your life?" *What about me?* she thought.

"My company doesn't need me anymore—it will do just fine being run by the capable people I've hired. And I can be involved when necessary. As for my life, I never truly had one. Now I do. And I have my brother back."

Liv sensed that was a load of BS. Roen had said his father was one of them and that they'd had to run from him. He'd also said he didn't want to ruin Liv's life in the same way. But couldn't he see that he was ruining her life in another way? Maybe she could get him to see that staying on that island would make all of his fears come true. That place was insanity.

Liv cleared her throat again. "I can't say I understand your attachment to that frightening place, Roen, and I'm beyond relieved you're okay, but please don't tell me you condone what's happening to those women."

He didn't speak, but instead responded with that fierce gaze.

"You *can't* be serious," she scoffed. "You turn them into vicious animals."

"They are not animals. They are sacred guardians of the island's waters."

"I watched them eat a man alive."

He stared at the floor for a moment and nodded his head. "Well, I'm sorry you had to see that."

"Sorry?" she seethed. "You're sorry? Roen, what's being done to those women is a crime. They're taken against their will and—"

"You're a landlover, Liv. You wouldn't understand."

"I understand perfectly fine. You've been drinking the Kool-Aid, and it somehow enables you to justify some pretty horrific stuff."

"There's no room for morality in this story, Liv. It's about survival. We do what we have to do."

"That's not a reason, Roen. You know it's not," she seethed.

"That island is alive, Liv. It thinks, it sees, it feels. And it's our job to protect it. She is the ocean's heart. She created all life and every life since then."

"The island is God? Okay."

"Not God. More like…an energy. But hers enables life to exist. Her water, her blood, flows into the ocean, and each and every drop of water on the planet holds a tiny piece of her. Which means she's a part of every living animal on this planet."

"You're saying we're all infected?"

"If being alive is considered an illness, I suppose, yes."

Liv simply looked at Roen, wondering what happened to him after she left the island. It was abundantly clear that he believed every word of what he'd just said.

Liv cleared her throat again. "Let's assume for a moment that I believe you, and the island is keeping us all alive—"

"No. She doesn't keep us alive. Think of her water as a catalyst that creates a spark in the early stages of life—at the point when cells form into the heart muscle. But to get that heart to beat, it needs a jolt of energy. From her."

Liv reached forward, grabbed her wine, threw it back, and then set it down again. "Uh… Okay… That's a very different spin on the whole reproduction thing."

"Think what you like, but without her, there would be no life on this planet. No humans, no animals. Nothing."

Liv's mind tried to digest the possibility that the island was some sort of microscopic defibrillator. Fact was, she already knew there were examples—many—of things in this world that existed, yet couldn't be seen. Love was one of them. So maybe, just maybe, what Roen said wasn't so crazy. Sure, some might call what he described the hand of God, others might call it nature's divine wisdom or biochemistry—didn't really matter. Something flipped the switch and turned us from a cluster of cells into a sophisticated organism with a beating heart. All that said, she still didn't want Roen to be a part of that place. He was a good man who deserved a home and love and…

Me.

"Did the island tell you all this herself?" Liv had a very difficult time imagining the two of them just sitting around, chatting about molecular biology over a cup of coffee.

"My people keep records and several world-renowned scientists live on the island to study her and help keep her healthy, which grows harder to do every year. The oceans are growing toxic, and every year she produces less and less water."

Liv would need a very, very long time for any of this to truly sink in and decide how much she believed. Nevertheless… "None of what you said explains what you're doing to those women."

"They're insurance, Liv. The island is afraid, and when people are afraid, they do what they must to survive."

Liv rubbed her face and sighed. "I still don't understand."

"Neither did I at first, but this is what I've been doing these last few months. Understanding, sifting through centuries of legends and folklore to get to the truth."

"Which is?" she said.

"It all has to change. That's why I'm really there. Our ancestors once lived exclusively in the ocean. Then one day, they grew tired of watching after the island and decided to explore the world. Our folklore says the island brought them back, then took away their fins and gave them legs to keep them from leaving. Soon after, they learned to build boats and tried to escape again. The island had to come up with another plan. She knew that the men of our kind were fiercely protective of our women and would never leave them willingly. So she changed the women back into creatures of the sea, this time making them nocturnal, unable to endure exposure to sunlight. Without the ability to swim in daylight, the women can't get far and must seek shelter from the light in the underwater caves that run beneath the island."

Liv blinked at Roen, trying to take it all in. *Don't start crying hysterically. Don't start crying hysterically. Maybe Roen isn't crazy...* Fact was, she'd seen the women's reaction to the sun—like damned aquatic vampires or something—but there'd been one who hadn't reacted to the light.

"Obviously," Roen continued, "the men protested and stopped drinking the water. We began growing old and dying off, so the island had to strike a compromise. We would conceive children on the island so that she could ensure they would be male—warriors—bound to her. And when those children grew up and returned, they'd take their father's place and he'd have his woman returned to him as she once was. They'd be free to leave."

If any, *any* of this fantasy were true, then it sounded more like a hostage situation.

"So the men serve dutifully," she said, "hoping their women will be given back. You understand how all of this is crazy, right?"

"I do." He took a sip of his wine. "The problem is that the island didn't keep her word. Not yet, anyway. Shortly after my people agreed to her terms, the island was invaded by Spanish explorers looking for the Fountain of Youth. We were unprepared and outnumbered, so we lost control of the island. If it weren't for the women—who picked them off one by one—we would never have taken it back. The name the Spanish explorers gave the island, El Corazón, serves as a reminder to all of us of what could happen if we let our guard down."

"Okay," Liv said. "You got the island back. So why didn't the island keep her word?"

"She says she'll honor the agreement as soon as she feels safe again and the numbers of those who protect her are big enough. She's been saying that for over five hundred years—and we have double the amount of men and maids."

"I'm guessing your people aren't so happy about that."

"We are divided," Roen said. "Some want to stay and protect the island. Others, especially the older ones, are at the end of their ropes. They believe that the island will never give us back our women, that she wants to keep everyone enslaved. Then there are those who believe in the scriptures—records of visions from our departed ones—which tell of a civil war. The island will lose its hold over us and be forced to set our women free. Some simply want it all to end so they can be reunited with the women they love in the afterlife."

"What do you believe?" Liv asked.

"I believe the world has changed. We have access to defense technology, laws to prevent trespassing, and people who might protect her willingly. But until we secure the island and make her feel safe, she'll continue demanding we have more children. And the women who turn out to be our mates will continue being turned into those creatures you saw."

Liv had thought that island was scary the moment she stepped foot there. But now, she thought the island was downright ruthless. Those poor women, the creatures, were the island's leverage to ensure the men didn't leave and did what she wanted, including making more warriors to protect her. The island dangled the carrot and the men hopped.

"That's why you're planning to renovate—or whatever," Liv said.

"Yes. I'm going to change things. But I have to do it carefully, in a way that won't create the wrong reaction. The island is like a frightened child who knows everything, but doesn't have the maturity to put it all into perspective. Her weakness is that she needs us. Our weakness is that we—humans included—need her."

Liv wasn't sure how much of this she believed, but Roen intended this conversation to lead somewhere. "Why are you telling me all this?"

Roen set down his glass and rubbed his chin. "Did you break your promise and tell someone about us?"

"Yes."

"Why, Liv?"

She looked away. She didn't want to say the truth. It was too painful.

"Why?" he yelled, causing her to jump in her seat. "She let you go. She let you walk away. Do you have any fucking idea what I gave up in return?"

So the island had used Liv as leverage against Roen? "That was why you stayed, wasn't it?"

He looked toward the fireplace, the muscles in his jaw pulsing. "Yes."

God. This was worse than she feared. Liv suspected something made him stay, but she'd hoped it was something weak and easily breakable. Or perhaps, something having to do with Lyle. But him giving up his life simply because he wanted to keep her safe wasn't what she wanted. Seeing someone you love suffer is a tragedy. Seeing someone you love suffer because of you is hell.

"After you left that room," he said, "she told me she knew I was letting you leave, and she'd planned to punish me for it by hurting you. But I put my foot down. Lyle and I are the last Dorans in existence, and I promised her there would be no more if she touched you."

So Roen stood up to her. Of course he would. Roen didn't take shit from anyone.

"What did she say?" Liv asked.

"She agreed to let you go, but only if I agreed to hold a Collection."

"I don't know what that is," Liv said.

"It's when we…" Roen took a short breath, "go to land and find women to bring back to the island."

"To claim," Liv said disapprovingly.

"Yes. Some will become maids and some—"

"Will become mothers." Liv couldn't believe this. But his story explained why that man attacked her as she left the island. It also explained why those things suddenly came to her rescue—a bargain had been struck. "I-I don't know what to say." Liv ran her hands through her hair. It sounded like the island got what it wanted. "Other than you had no right to barter with the lives of others, or your own, just to save me."

Roen shook his head remorsefully. "Why wouldn't I have? It was a simple deal. As long as you kept your end of the bargain—to never tell—and I kept mine, you'd be safe."

"How's any of this simple?"

"The Collection would've happened eventually. And I would have stayed regardless."

"Why?" she asked, her heart pounding away with volatile emotion. "Why would you want to stay there?"

"You are not safe around me. We're like poison, Liv."

"How can you say that?" Roen was anything but poison. That island, on the other hand...

"I watched what happens to women who stay with my kind. It eats them away, drives them mad with grief. I'd never let that happened to you, regardless of how much I want you. So in the end, I gave up nothing I wouldn't have given anyway. But you had to tell, didn't you?"

So he'd thrown in the towel before they'd ever had a chance, which deeply wounded her. He simply didn't understand what he meant to her.

"I needed help, Roen. You have no idea what I've gone through. The media's been looking everywhere for you. People think you were kidnapped and I helped. Your own fucking lawyer has been harassing me. But, of course, they didn't believe me when I told them I didn't even know you, because *you* called them. *You* told them to come get me, but you were nowhere to be found."

"You should've kept your mouth shut."

"I tried. I really did," she said angrily. "I didn't say a word to the FBI, who detained me for two days. And I didn't say anything to my family. Do you know how hard it is to look them in the eyes and lie? They know me. They know I'm hiding something. Even Dana and Krista, my own two sisters, won't speak to me because they think I don't trust them. My life has fallen apart, Roen. I have no privacy, the press keeps printing stories that say I'm a criminal, and I can't go back to school! But I could've handled all that, Roen, I really could've if I didn't see your face every time I closed my eyes. I thought when I left you behind, I'd sentenced you to death because those creatures made me promise I wouldn't tell anyone about the island. Which meant I couldn't send help for you. Which meant I couldn't live with myself."

Roen glared at her for a moment and then stood and walked over to the kitchen where he'd left the open bottle of wine on the counter.

He poured a generous glass, gulped it down, and then shot her a look. "All you needed to do was to live and move the fuck on, woman."

He just doesn't get it. "That's the point. I couldn't!" she yelled. "I can't!"

Roen planted both arms on the counter and dropped his head. "I'm a fucking bastard who's never cared about anyone aside from Lyle and my mother. I use people, step on them, exploit their weaknesses for my own gain. I've made billions destroying other people's companies, and I never gave a damn. I still don't. And when it comes to women, I've fucked hundreds and don't remember their names. Not because I can't, but because I couldn't give a shit about any of them."

"What's your goddamned point, Roen? That I'm stupid for caring about you?"

"Yes."

She stood and walked over to the granite kitchen island, stopping directly across from him and dipping her head, hoping he'd look up and see the sincerity in her eyes.

"I think you've got it backwards," she said calmly. "I'm not stupid. I'm the only one who's ever been brave enough to care about you." No bones about it, Roen was intimidating as hell, and his icy exterior sent a clear message: don't be foolish enough to care about me, because I won't care back. Which is why Liv could only assume that the women he'd slept with probably never gave a crap about him—not the real him, anyway. How could they? *Why* would they? Roen had a reputation, and anyone who picked up a tabloid knew it. But the truth was, Roen was the kind of guy who pushed people away, so all they saw was some hot, wealthy guy they could bolster their own egos with. They'd fucked Roen Doran—something to tell their friends, perhaps. Something to elevate their own statuses. At the end of the day, they'd be foolish to expect anything else out of the relationship. Unless they were willing to chisel through all those layers of ice and take the time to really see him for who he was. Strong. Defiant. Beautiful.

"Roen, you see yourself as the aggressor, but those women used you, too. They fucked you and let you leave. I'm guessing not one of them lifted a finger to keep you, call you, or learn a thing about you because you were nothing more than a conquest."

With a rage-red face, Roen shot her an embittered look, but didn't speak.

"If you want to get angry, then go ahead," she said. "But don't ever call me stupid for wanting you. You put your life on the line and risked everything to save me—a stranger. And when someone like me—who knows damned well they're worth something, with a pretty damned high IQ, I'd like to add—says they can't forget someone like you, take that as a fucking compliment."

Roen stared for several long moments. "She wants me to kill you, Liv," he blurted out.

Liv inhaled deeply. "You're going to kill me?"

Okay. Maybe I am stupid.

"No. She wants me to kill you, and I refused. I told her that if she lays a finger on you, it's over. I won't help her. I'll let them come for her."

"Who? Who will come for her?"

"She thinks..." He ran his hands through his thick brown hair. "She thinks the landlovers are coming soon. She says she's watched the event in her dreams. They come. They start stealing her water."

"I don't understand."

"The water she produces keeps her alive, too. And just like when you give blood, you can only donate so much at once. Otherwise you'll die. But what she can spare, she gives to the ocean and to us."

"So she thinks that people are coming to take it all away?"

"Yes. She says the end is near. First they find her, then they drain her dry, and she dies. The rest of the world is gone shortly after."

If that were true, then the island couldn't afford to lose anyone—at least, she'd see it that way. *I can't believe I'm talking about the island like she's alive.*

"So what happens if you don't...?" Liv really didn't want to say the words "kill me."

"I honestly don't know at this point, but I do know I can't risk seeing you again. Maybe if she knows you're out of my life, she'll leave you alone. But you can't tell anyone else about her or me, Liv. Not anyone."

"I wouldn't tell—"

Roen gave her a sharp look.

"Okay. I told my psychiatrist, but that was different. I was trying to survive, trying to figure out how the hell I could live without..." Her voice trailed off. "You."

There was a long moment of silence before Roen spoke. "It can't happen. You deserve to live a real life, not some distorted version of love like my mother and father had."

She still didn't know the whole story of what his father had done, but this wasn't the time to go there. She did know, however, that he'd caused Roen a great amount of pain. "You wouldn't hurt me, Roen. You're not your father."

"No, I'm not. Because I will do what's right for you," he said.

"Meaning this is goodbye." He wanted her far away from him and that island.

"Yes," he replied curtly.

Liv held back her tears. She didn't want to accept any of this. Most of all, she didn't want to let him go. She'd waited her entire life to meet a man like him, and she knew she never would again. There was only one Roen Doran, and he'd somehow become a part of her.

"What if you're successful?" she asked. "What if you convince the island she's safe? Then will you leave?"

He shook his head no. "A group of us will need to remain with her always. But hopefully it won't be many and we'll all be there of our own free will."

She couldn't accept this, but arguing with the man wasn't going to change his mind. And frankly, she was too heartbroken to fight anymore. She just wanted to leave because looking at him hurt too much.

"Roen, just promise you'll help those women and stop bringing new ones to the island."

"I can't promise that, Liv. I've already made a deal with the island. For you."

"Then break your promise," Liv argued. "I don't want to live if it means a bunch of women are...are..." She didn't even know what to call it.

"Another Collection was inevitable either way. Things have been done a certain way for a very long time and change doesn't happen overnight. But I promise no one will come to that island who doesn't want to be there."

Liv knew that was only half of the story. Because while those men might convince a woman to go to the island of her own free will, they were in the dark about what happened next. "You trick them, Roen."

"Until my people are free from this nightmare and the island is safe from landlovers, I'm not in a position to change things." Roen stared with his piercing green eyes.

"But..." Liv abandoned her thought. It didn't matter if she believed his entire story; he believed it. And he believed he was keeping her safe along with everyone else.

Maybe he is. And maybe it's not your battle. That's what she told herself, but really, her heart was slowly cracking, and she didn't want him to see it happen.

"Well"—Liv swallowed her sadness—"I guess this is goodbye." She glanced across the kitchen island at Roen once again, but his expression gave nothing away.

Roen cleared his throat. "I believe it is. Edward will see you back to the plane and home. By morning, the media will be off your back, as I plan to hold a press conference shortly. Goodbye, Liv."

Liv gave a quick nod and started walking to the door. *Don't turn around. Don't look at him. Just leave. Just leave. Just go outside, and you'll be okay.*

"Liv." Roen was right behind her when she reached for the door, his deep voice filled with irritation or anger or...something. "I'm not happy about any of this either. I don't think I ever will be after meeting you and knowing you won't be in my life."

Don't turn around. Don't turn around.

Liv reached for the door handle. "Thanks for everything, Roen."

She suddenly felt Roen's strong hands on her shoulders. Then his lips on the side of her neck and the warmth of his chest pressing against her back. His touch made her whole body ache and weep. It sucked to feel something so wonderful, knowing it wasn't meant to be and that she'd never have it again.

Roen's hands slid down to her waist, and he wrapped his arms tightly around her. "Thank you, Liv," he whispered. "Thank you for being the only woman ever brave enough to love me."

The tears began welling in her eyes, and her heart caved in. If she didn't go now, she'd end up doing something she regretted. Like begging him to stay with her. *He'd only say no and make this even more painful.*

She held her breath tightly, attempting to cling to her sanity. Then he released his grip and reached around her to open the door. Avoiding eye contact, she stepped out into the hallway, feeling like her body was made from eggshells in the process of cracking into a million tiny pieces. One tap and she'd disintegrate into nothing.

She glanced over her shoulder at Roen standing in the doorway, and when she saw the pained look in his eyes, it undid her. She rushed toward him and their mouths collided. His sensual lips and silky tongue moved against hers, and his kiss felt like the only thing in her life that had ever truly made sense. And the heat of his sweet breath mixing with hers, his scent filling her lungs, was like a drug made from concentrated sin.

He turned their bodies, putting her back against the wall. With his large size and height she felt completely shielded from the world around them, it was just him and her and their mouths moving together, their tongues sliding in a desperate frenzy.

Then his body began buzzing with that strange energy, and he leaned into her, his hands feverishly moving over her breasts and down to cup her ass.

"God, I want you, Liv." He returned to kissing her for a moment. "I can't get the taste of you out of my mind."

She felt the same way.

Roen ground against her; meanwhile her hands reached around him, seeking out his hard ass, wanting to feel the muscles flex beneath her palms. In her mind, she saw the two of them naked, their bodies moving together in desperate need, while Roen pumped his hard cock inside her. It was the same erotic image she'd seen night after night since she'd left the island. And if this was the end of the road for them, then she wanted to know what it was like just once. She wanted to feel him over her, in her, holding her down as he thrust his thick, long shaft as deeply as it could go. More than that, however, she just wanted more time to know every piece of him—even the parts she couldn't see inside his heart and soul.

She broke the kiss and looked up at him. "Roen?" she whispered, her heart beating at a million miles per second. "I'm asking."

He flashed a sinful, seductive little smile with that sensual mouth of his, but in the space of one second, all emotion drained from his face, and his eyes seemed to turn a deeper shade of green. Hate, fury, bitterness reflected back at her.

"And my answer is no." He stepped away as if she were poison.

Liv blinked. *Wait. What just happened?*

"You were wrong," he said. "You're not strong. You're weak. I need a woman I can fuck and won't break, who can raise my sons and won't get in my way. That or she must be able to protect the island. You're not good for either."

Liv felt mortified. Down to the marrow in her bones. "Is that you talking or that fucking psycho-bitch?"

Roen raised his hand to slap her. "Don't ever, *ever* speak of the island or of me again. If you do, there will be no mercy. Understand, landlover?"

Liv didn't raise her own hands in defense. She would never cower from a man. She would never allow someone to bully her or try to control her like that.

"You done?" Her eyes stuck to his hard gaze, challenging him back.

He laughed sadistically and lowered his hand. "Leave. Scurry back to your little human life. Just remember who gave it to you. And never forget who can take it away."

Liv glared at Roen. Or the island. Or whoeverthefuck really spoke. "My *parents* gave me life. And they would never try to hurt or use me. Can't say the same for you or your island, Roen. Goodbye."

She turned and headed for the elevator, poking the call button. Within a few moments, the doors opened, and she stepped inside. This time, she wouldn't look at him. Never again.

☙❧

"Sonofabitch. Who does he think he is?" Liv said from the backseat of the limo heading down the nearly vacant highway toward the SeaTac airport.

"Our leader," replied the driver, who she'd learned was named Edward.

"Not *my* leader," she grumbled. At least out of all this, those psycho Neanderthals weren't coming for her. She hoped. And now that she knew Roen was free, she had closure. *Yeah, free to be a complete asshole.* She could finally move past this chapter of her life.

With the pent-up emotions inside, tears began streaming down her face. She wiped underneath her eyes. *You're safe now, Liv. You're safe.*

Yeah. And Roen bartered with the island again to get it. Her mouth fell open as she mentally stepped back from the situation. He wouldn't go out of his way to protect her if he didn't really have feelings for her.

He didn't mean it. He didn't mean any of it. He just wanted her to leave. Liv felt ashamed for what she'd said and not seeing right through his little ploy, but…

She shook her head. He wasn't faking it. She was good at reading people—their posture, facial expressions, breathing—Roen had been dead serious about what he'd said. It was like when he was on the island and had become this other version of himself.

Did it really matter? It was over. She would never see him again, and he didn't want anything to do with her. That much she knew.

The scariest part was that his little story about that island being more than just an island was plausible. The little things she'd seen and felt supported it. Hell, the minute she'd shared the word "mermen" with her psychiatrist, it was like the salt water in her veins began punishing her.

Liv's phone began beeping, and she dug it from her purse. Her mother's cell phone number popped up on the screen. It was now almost three thirty in the morning. She answered. "Mom? What's wrong?"

"Livvy, Dana's in the emergency room."

Oh no. "What happened?"

"Steve doesn't know. He said she started having problems breathing, and he called nine-one-one."

Steve was Dana's boyfriend. They'd been living together in Wrangell for the last few years.

"Your father and I are pulling up to the emergency room."

Liv had just been to that hospital. "I'm…I'm…" How could she explain being out of town? She couldn't. "I'm in Seattle right now, but I'll be there as soon as I can."

"Seattle? Why didn't you say anything? Did you go to see your professor?"

Liv's sociology professor had been hounding Liv to return and finish her PhD, but with everything going on, Liv didn't think it would be possible.

"Something like that," Liv replied. "I'll explain later." When she could figure out a good excuse. "Keep me posted. I'll be there as soon as I can."

CHAPTER FOURTEEN

Three hours later, Liv ran through the automatic sliding doors into the small ER waiting room. She immediately spotted Steve and her dad. Her father, an insurance broker, was a thin man with thick glasses and short, curly gray hair. Steve worked for the Department of Fish and Game, but looked like he belonged on the beach with his shaggy, dirty blond hair.

"Where is she?" Liv asked.

Her dad shook his head. "Why haven't you been answering your phone? We were worried sick about you."

"Uh…" Liv blinked. She'd used up the battery on the flight home to read the breaking news about Roen having resurfaced. He would be holding a news conference this morning. "My phone died. How is she?"

"Stable. Your mom is with her now. The doctor's still running tests."

"What happened?" she asked Steve, whose brown eyes were bloodshot like he'd been crying.

"I don't know," Steve replied. "We were sleeping, and I heard her scream, and then she started convulsing and couldn't breathe."

Liv felt the floor drop out beneath her. Steve and her father grabbed her quickly, one of them managing to push her into a chair.

"Livvy, are you all right?" her dad asked. "Steve, go get her some water."

Steve scrambled off while her father crouched in front of her.

"I'm okay," Liv said. "Just—it's been a long day, and the shock of Dana and…"

Fuck. Was this some sort of punishment? Because what Steve described was exactly like what had happened yesterday to her.

"I need to see Dana. I need to talk to her," Liv said.

"Only one visitor at a time, but your mother will be out shortly—"

"Dad, I need to see her. *Now.*"

He gave her a strange look. "Okay. I'll show you where she is." They walked to the admitting nurse, who waved them in. Apparently, she was too busy yelling at some man about his bad manners and bothering another nurse. In a small town like this, where most everyone knew or knew of everyone else, rules weren't always so important. Being polite, however, was.

They walked past several empty beds and curtain dividers to a spot at the very end. Liv spotted her mother sitting beside Dana, who was lying down, her long dark-brown hair a matted mess. Thankfully, Dana's big brown eyes were open and alert. And, ironically, she was staring up at a muted TV stuck to the wall, with Roen's picture on it.

Like she'd done for the past three hours, Liv took her pain and shoved it down a dark hole somewhere deep inside. "Dana? How are you feeling?"

"Hey, Livvy," Dana said in a perky voice. "Did you hear the news? Mr. Sexy is alive. God, that man is so hot. Can I have one for Christmas, Mom?"

Their mother, who had the same brown hair and eyes as Liv and her sisters, looked at her and then back at Dana, shaking her head. "Her breathing's stable. The doctor thinks it might've been an asthma attack."

Dana didn't have asthma. In fact, she and her sisters were healthy as horses when it came to that sort of stuff.

Her sister smiled weakly. "I'm fine, Livvy. Just go home. I'm sure whatever it was, it's just a fluke."

Fluke. It was too much of a coincidence to be a fluke. If that goddamned island had anything to do with this, she'd burn that damn hunk of rock down to the ground.

Are you listening to yourself, Liv? You sound like Roen. The island wasn't alive.

Just like mermaids aren't real?

"And tell Krista not to come," Dana added. Krista was their older sister, who lived in Portland.

"Ma'am, only one visitor at a time, so I'm afraid two of you will have to go," said the nurse, who slipped by Liv and started checking Dana's IV.

Liv's mother stood. "I need to go to the little girls' room. You can keep Dana company." She walked away with Liv's dad, and the nurse hurried off to the next patient, leaving them alone.

"Dana, I have to ask you something." Liv took her mother's seat beside Dana and placed her purse on the floor. "When you couldn't breathe, do you remember feeling like your veins were burning?"

Dana nodded. "Yeah. And then it traveled to my lungs. How did you know?"

Liv couldn't tell her the truth. "It happened to me once. A long time ago."

"Ms. Stratton, you're back." Dr. Fuller stood at the foot of Dana's bed with a surprised look. "How are you feeling?"

"Uhhh...Dr. Fuller. You're still here." Liv glanced at Dana and then plastered on a fake smile.

"I'm covering for another doctor with a lovely double shift," Dr. Fuller explained. "How are you feeling?"

"Great. I'm just here visiting my sister," Liv replied.

"Why is she asking about you?" Dana glared at Liv.

"I wasn't feeling so great yesterday," Liv said, but Dana gave her that look; she knew Liv was lying. She always knew. It was the reason that they hadn't spoken in over a month.

"Well," the doctor said to Dana, "it appears you had an allergic reaction to something. A food allergy."

"I'm not allergic to any foods," Dana said.

"Sometimes these things come on late in life. Your histamine levels are elevated and you had all of the symptoms of anaphylactic shock. Earlier, you said you weren't stung or bitten, but did you eat peanuts or any kind of shellfish today?"

"We had crab rolls for dinner," Dana answered.

"The likely culprit," said the doctor. "I'll put in a referral to the allergy clinic so we can know for certain. In the meantime, I'm sending you home with some antihistamines."

"Thank you, Doctor," Dana said. As soon as she disappeared, Dana looked at Liv. "What the hell is going on with you?"

Liv hated lying, but she wasn't about to step over that line again. No matter how much or little she believed Roen's story. "I really don't want to talk about it."

"Liv, I'm your sister. Why do you keep shutting me out?"

"I'm not. And we shouldn't be talking about this right now. You need to rest."

"I'm fine," Dana growled, "and there is nothing more important to me than you guys—you know that. What the hell is going on? Are you in trouble? Did something happen to you on that fishing boat?"

Liv shook her head no, but her eyes couldn't help flashing to that damned TV screen, where a small picture of Roen's handsome face, pre-island, was displayed in a little box while two reporters chatted away. Roen's short, thick caramel brown hair was combed neatly back, and he was displaying a charming smile with a little dimple puckering in each cheek. Why hadn't she ever noticed them? *He is so damned beautiful.*

Liv's heart began to free-fall. How would she ever get over him?

"Stop looking at the hot man on the TV, Liv, and tell me what's going on."

Liv wasn't about to start spilling her guts about Roen or the island; however, the words, "He's mine," popped into her mind.

Dana started to gasp and began clawing at her throat as if choking.

"Dana!" Liv screamed. "Ohmygod. Dana!" Liv jumped up and yelled, but when she looked out down the hall, the nurse and Dr. Fuller were rushing to an elderly man who was being wheeled in by two paramedics. "Help! My sister can't breathe."

The doctor flashed a look her way and then told the nurse to page Dr. Silverton at home.

"It's okay, Dana," Liv said, rushing over to her sister, trying to get her to calm down. But Dana's body began to buck uncontrollably on the gurney, and her face was turning blue.

"Ohmygod. Don't die, Dana. Don't die."

Dr. Fuller appeared and began pulling supplies and tubes from a small cabinet in the corner. "Goddammit!" Obviously, something was missing.

The doctor looked at Liv. "Keep her calm. I'll be back in two seconds."

Calm? "Dana, honey, just hang on." Dana's terrified face was completely blue now, her mouth wide open trying to get air. Liv's eyes gravitated toward her purse sitting on the floor. The corner of her floral makeup bag stuck out, and that's when she remembered the vial of water. The creature on the island had ripped it from the man's neck and thrown it at her. Liv never used it—was too afraid, she supposed—but she'd ended up keeping the thing. Why? She didn't know, but throwing away something like that seemed wrong.

Because it could save a person's life from just about anything. Liv practically dove for her purse and snatched the makeup bag, pouring out the contents onto the gurney between Dana's legs. She spotted the small vial and grabbed it.

"Hold on, Dana. Hold on." Hands shaking, Liv uncorked the miniature, test-tube-shaped vial and separated Dana's lips, pouring it into her mouth. "Drink, Dana. Drink it."

Dana sputtered and hacked, but it looked like some went down. Dana's entire body froze, and in less than three seconds Dana gasped, this time taking a full breath.

"Dana, Dana, can you hear me?" Liv whispered, and Dana's panicked brown eyes set on Liv. "You can't tell anyone. Do you understand? You can't tell anyone I gave you something, and you can't ever ask me what it was. Do you understand?"

Dana just stared in terror.

"Please, Dana. You have to trust me. I'd never do anything to hurt you, but you can't ever—"

"Okay, Dana. I'm going to…" A panicked Dr. Fuller stood at the foot of Dana's bed, holding some plastic parts in her hand.

Oh crap. "I think she's okay now." Liv tried to sound as shocked as the doctor looked.

Dr. Fuller sat next to Dana and placed her stethoscope on her chest. Dana sucked in several breaths and released them.

"Sounds all clear." She took out her penlight and a tongue depressor. "Say ah."

Dana still panted, but managed to produce the sound.

"No obstruction." The doctor stood and then looked at Liv. "I don't understand."

Liv shrugged.

"I think it felt like a panic attack," Dana mumbled.

The doctor glanced back at Dana, whose face was flushed. "We'll keep her the rest of the day and run some more tests. In the meantime, I think it's best we let her rest. Alone."

Liv reached to hug Dana goodbye, but she shirked away.

Liv dropped her hands. "See you later, Dana. Glad you're feeling better." She left the ER, not bothering to say goodbye to her parents. The guilt was too much. It felt like the entire situation was all her fault—despite the insanity of that thought.

CHAPTER FIFTEEN

Three weeks later. Wrangell, Alaska

After saying goodbye to Roen that night, Liv could honestly say this chapter of her life was closed—not forgotten, but closed. Roen was no longer haunting her dreams, and he'd made a public appearance, which every news channel and newspaper covered. The speculation surrounding whether or not he was still alive shifted to stories that questioned his health. Only, he looked healthier and more beautiful than ever, a fact the media completely ignored. Because why else would someone like Roen Doran simply step down and turn his multibillion dollar company over to another person after a mysterious absence?

The media frenzy lasted about one week; meanwhile Liv started picking up the pieces of her life—well, making plans to do so, anyway— including trying to let go of her feelings for Roen.

But that wasn't going to happen until time put distance between them.

In the meantime, she planned to return to Washington State to finish her doctorate in the fall. Given the situation with the shipwreck, the university had been very supportive about allowing her to restart her dissertation—just as her professor had promised. Her only challenge now was what theme she'd choose. Bonds, love, and relationships were topics she no longer wanted to think about.

As for her sister, Liv still hadn't spoken with Dana about the incident, though they had spoken. But Liv never planned to discuss the vial of water and hoped that Dana never brought it up. Liv didn't know if Dana's trip to the hospital was somehow connected to that island, but why take the risk? It was behind them. It was behind Liv.

And I'm never looking back. No matter what. She simply had to have faith that her heart would eventually heal.

Tonight, however, Liv looked forward to her parents' fortieth wedding anniversary, six months in the making. It had almost been called off several times, but now there was a hell of a lot to celebrate. Everyone was safe and together. That included family from five states who'd flown in, practically taking over the entire inn down the road not to mention her parents' four-bedroom house. It had been one hell of a busy week, spending time with her cousins and aunts and uncles, barbequing, going on fishing excursions, and dinners every night.

Liv hit the blinker of her mom's old gray Subaru—they kept it around for guests, which were always plentiful in the summer—and turned down the narrow residential street toward the marina. As she got closer to Bears and Brew, the restaurant slash pub overlooking the ocean where the party was being held, her palms began to sweat and her face felt hot. *Nerves. It's just nerves.*

Liv would give the speech tonight, which was why everyone went on ahead without her. She needed to practice a few times in silence.

I'm sure it will be fine, Liv thought to herself, trying to keep her breathing even. She parked on the street just a few doors down from the restaurant—a giant, glorified log cabin with a large ocean-side patio—and checked her makeup in the lighted vanity mirror. Her face was finally beginning to look normal again now that she'd put back some of the fifteen pounds she'd lost. It was amazing how quickly a girl could gain weight once carbs were reintroduced.

Liv freshened up her pink lip gloss and then petted the back of her dark hair, which she'd straightened into a silky mane. *Feels good to feel human again.* The not smelling like shark blood was great, too.

She opened the car door and stepped out into the cool evening air, smoothing down her red dress. It was the same one she'd worn for Christmas—modestly snug with an open back and spaghetti straps. She just hadn't had the energy to shop for a dress, and it was the only thing that fit.

She entered the restaurant and immediately felt more relaxed. A '50s rock band played—the only band in town— and she spotted her parents among the couples laughing and dancing on the floor. It was just like she'd imagined when she'd been fighting for her life on that island.

You made it. And you have so much to be grateful for.

"Hey, didn't you wear that at Christmas?" said a familiar voice.

Liv turned her head and saw Krista standing there in her famous little black dress. It was the only dress her sister owned and no one expected that to change. Krista—who looked like a slightly older version of Liv and Dana with long dark hair, pale skin, and big brown eyes—was a veterinarian for the Portland zoo, taking care of their marine mammals. So her usual attire was a wetsuit or galoshes and jeans.

"Ha. Look who's talking." Liv gave Krista a tight squeeze. "But as always, you look stunning."

"Thanks. You too," Krista replied.

"So did everyone make it?" Liv asked, her eyes sweeping the room and immediately spotting a few of their cousins from Texas, who had just flown in.

"Aunt Libby called and said she was sick, but I think everyone else is here. Plus a few uninvited guests."

Liv nodded and waved to her parents, who were in mid-twist.

"But I already told Mom I'd change tables so your date can sit with you," Krista added.

Liv's eyes snapped toward Krista. "Date? I didn't bring a date."

Krista gave her a strange look. "Are you sure? Because the guy asked for you and said you knew he was coming."

"No. I swear. I didn't invite anyone."

"Well, he's..." Krista's eyes searched the crowded room. "Oh! There he goes. He just went out to the patio."

Liv didn't see anyone. "What does he look like?"

"Hot. No wait. That's too low for him. God-like. Green eyes, well-built, shortish hair, and really tall—are you sure you don't want him, because I'll take him. The man nearly melted my panties off. Except I'm not wearing any. But if I had been, they'd be a puddle on the floor."

Roen's here? Liv's mind sparked with indescribable joy. Because while she'd been doing her best to get over him, there was a Grand Canyon-sized gap between being in healing mode and being fully healed. It would take Liv years, perhaps a lifetime, to really get over Roen. But now, if he was here, could that mean he'd solved his issues with the island or that he'd changed his mind about her?

The thought send her heart racing and her eyes filled with tears of hope.

"Um. I'll be right back," Liv said and began making her way through the crowd. She smiled and gave quick hugs to folks, promising to be right back after she took care of some "important" detail.

"Ms. Stratton, there you are," said a woman, stopping Liv halfway through the room.

It was Dr. Fuller from the ER. She wore a black blazer over a white fitted dress.

"Oh. Hi. I wasn't expecting to see you here." Liv's eyes gravitated toward the double doors leading outside, searching for any sign of Roen.

"Your mother invited me, and I couldn't say no."

Liv flashed a quick smile. "Well, it's really nice of you to come, but I need to talk to—"

Dr. Fuller grabbed Liv's forearm, applying a bit of pressure. "That's the thing, Liv. I need to talk to you."

"About what?"

"About what was in that vial," she replied with exaggerated sweetness.

Oh shit. "I don't know what you mean." Had she left the vial in the ER? Obviously, she had. With all the commotion, it must've slipped her mind.

"Don't bullshit me. I saw she was suffocating, and then I came back a few seconds later and she was all better. Then I found this on the floor." Dr. Fuller pulled the empty vial from the pocket of her black blazer. "Coincidentally, when I got the lab results back from your sister's blood, she had the same unidentifiable compound."

Liv shrugged. "Your lab probably had another glitch."

"No. I had her blood sent out to a lab in Ketchikan, right along with the sample I got from the tube."

Liv felt her spit stick in her throat. "I don't know what to tell you. The vial just had holy water in it. That's all. I must've dropped it, and it spilled." That was a terrible lie. Who the hell would believe she ran around with holy water in her purse? She wasn't some Catholic priest. Hell, she wasn't even Catholic.

That said, there were no other choices.

The doctor gave her a look. "That wasn't water."

Liv stared at her, wondering the obvious: what the hell was this doctor going to do?

"I'm sorry, Dr. Fuller," Liv said, "but I'm not sure what your point is or why you're—"

"Because—and I know it's going to sound crazy—but I dreamed of you coming into my ER. I dreamed of you and that water and of it being a cure for every illness that's ever plagued mankind."

Whatthehell? Liv had no clue what was going on, but… *I can't deal with this right now!* Roen was there for some reason and she could only hope it was to answer her prayers.

"You're right," Liv said. "That does sound crazy. If you'll excuse me, I have people to say hi to."

Liv headed toward the double doors, her mind scrambling, attempting to deal with the fact that Roen had showed up. She pushed outside onto the dimly lit patio overlooking the marina. A cigarette butt smoldered in a standing ashtray next to the cement bench where she spotted the silhouette of a broad-shouldered man in a black suit. Liv felt her heart thumping and adrenaline shooting through her veins.

"Roen?" She could scarcely believe her eyes.

Roen slowly stood and turned around. "I'm not Roen."

Liv's jaw dropped and panic replaced her mixed emotions. "Shane?"

His green eyes caught the light behind her and glittered with the fierce determination of a predator about to make a kill.

"Hello, Liv," he said in a menacing tone. "Nice to see you again." No, it didn't matter that he was in a suit, or his hair was neatly combed back and cut shorter. He wasn't a civilized man with civilized intentions.

Liv turned and reached for the doors to run inside.

"I wouldn't do that if I were you," Shane said. "Not when so many people you care about are inside. And I'm sure you'd hate for them to get dragged into this."

Liv froze with her hand on the handle and then looked at him. "What do you want?"

Shane flashed a wicked grin. "The Collection has begun. And I've come to claim what's mine." He lunged and covered her scream with his hand before dragging her over the railing into the cold water.

TO BE CONTINUED...

NOTE FROM AUTHOR

Hi everyone!

I knoooow… It's the dreaded cliffhanger I'm so famous for. (The good news is that it means more is coming!) But, as always, there's a method to my mermadness. Obviously, I won't spoil what comes next, but you know how I love twists, and Roen's journey is just getting started.

ANYWAY, if you're looking for more, Book #2, MerMadmen is AVAILABLE NOW!

BUY LINKS & EXCERPT can be found at: **www.mimijean.net/mermadmen.html**

ALSO if you would like an awesome SIGNED MERMEN BOOKMARK, please shoot me a note (contact info is in the back). It's first come, first serve, but if I've got 'em, it's yours! You can always check my website:

mimijean.net/romance_adventure_gear.html

for swag availability, too.

DON'T FORGET! IF YOU LOVED the story and take the time to WRITE A REVIEW (which us authors so, so, sooooo appreciate!) please let me know when you request your bookmark. I have special "thank you" swag for the first few hundred.

And KING FANS…Heads up! Don't miss the big cover reveal in the back!

HAPPY READING!

Mimi

P.S. I know some of you enjoy hearing my writer's playlist. It's now posted on:

www.mimijean.net/mermen1.html

ACKNOWLEDGMENTS

A HUUUGE thank you to my MER-licious crew of helpers who swam with me across the finish line on this crazy-ass book. Kylie, Dali, Layota, Su, and Pauline. Words can't express how grateful I am for your support, so I'll simply make a gurgling sound which means "thank you" in mermaid speak.

I'd also like to thank Jan at Author Sidekick for helping me keep the wheels on the bus with all of the important non-writing stuff like making hottie banners and booking ads!

And needless to say, my undying gratitude goes to my guys. Every day is a challenge, and your hugs and kisses are always there to push me on.

He never wanted this. He only wanted her.

EVERYTHING ABOUT THE ISLAND OF EL CORÁZON IS WRONG. The men are ruthless warriors who call themselves mermen but don't have any fish parts, the island isn't exactly an island, and the women...well, let's just say their story isn't pretty. More like a nightmare. Which is exactly why billionaire Roen Doran will do anything to protect the woman he can't live without from that violent place. Including becoming the island's leader and giving her up forever.

WHEN LIV STRATTON ESCAPED THAT TERRIFYING ISLAND in the North Pacific after being shipwrecked, she didn't just leave behind the horror, she left behind Roen Doran. A man she didn't know, but who risked everything to save her. And now her heart can't seem to move on. So part of her wonders if it's somehow her fault she's been taken against her will and locked inside a ship bound for El Corazón. But an even bigger part wonders if Roen will lift a finger to save her this time. After all, now he's one of them…

FOR AN EXCERPT GO TO:

www.mimijean.net/mermen1.html

MACK. COMING SPRING 2016

**His truth won't break you.
It will tear your heart to pieces.**

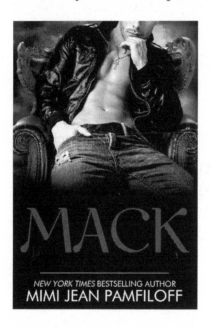

KING TRILOGY AUDIOBOOK

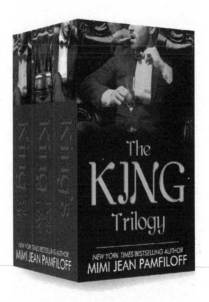

King Trilogy Available in Audiobook

KING'S – March 31, 2015

KING FOR A DAY – April 21, 2015

KING OF ME – May 12, 2015

Find Buy Links at:

mimijean.net/king_trilogy_books.html

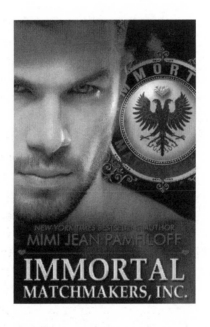

BECAUSE…dysfunctional immortals

need love, too.

ANDRUS

Once the most powerful immortal assassin ever to exist, this demigod now spends his days pining for the girl who got away: Helena. Doesn't help that

Made in the USA
Lexington, KY
22 December 2016

She continues to hope that her books will inspire a leather pants comeback (for men) and that she might make you laugh when you need it most.

Sign up for Mimi's mailing list
for giveaways and new release news!

LEARN MORE:

mailto: mimi@mimijean.net

www.mimijean.net

twitter.com/MimiJeanRomance

http://radioslot.com/show/mancandyshow/

www.facebook.com/MimiJeanPamfiloff

About The Author

 Mimi Jean Pamfiloff is a *New York Times* & *USA Today* best-selling author of Paranormal and Contemporary Romance. Her books have been #1 genre sellers around the world. Both traditionally and independently published, Mimi has sold over 500,000 books since publishing her first title in 2012, and she plans to spontaneously combust once she hits the one million mark. Although she obtained her international MBA and worked for over 15 years in the corporate world, she believes that it's never too late to come out of the romance closet and follow your dream.

When not screaming at her computer or hosting her very inappropriate radio show (*Man Candy Show* on Radioslot.com), Mimi spends time with her two pirates in training, her loco-for-the-chili-pepper Mexican hubby, and her rat terrier, DJ Princess Snowflake, in the San Francisco Bay Area.

he's also Helena's full-time nanny slash bodyguard. But now that the apocalypse is over and her husband, the vampire general, has returned home for good, it's time to move on.

But can Andrus let go of the woman he secretly loves?

Cimil, Goddess of the Underworld and owner of Immortal Matchmakers, Inc., knows the solution is finding another gal. The right gal. But getting a woman to date this callous, unrefined, coldhearted warrior will prove to be the biggest challenge of her existence. Good thing they're in L.A.

When aspiring actress Sadie Townsend finds herself one week away from being thrown out on the street, the call from her agent is like a gift from heaven. But when she learns the job is teaching the world's biggest barbarian how to act like a gentleman, she wonders if she shouldn't have asked for more money. He's vulgar, uncaring, and rougher around the edges than a serrated bread knife. He's also sexy, fierce, and undeniably tormented.

Will Sadie help him overcome his past, or will she find her heart hopelessly trapped by a man determined to self-destruct?

MORE INFO:

mimijean.net/immortal_matchmakers.html